PUFFIN

WILD CHILD AND OTHER STORIES

Paro Anand can't stop writing books for children, young adults and adults, although many people tell her she should slow down. She also works with children in schools and NGOs, through her programme Literature in Action. She is a world record holder for helping children make the World's Longest Newspaper. She performs her stories for all who will listen—in India and many parts of the world. She has been awarded for her contribution to children's literature by The Russian Centre for Science and Culture. On Republic Day 2007 Dr Kalam, the President of India, honoured her for her writing. Her book, *No Guns at My Son's Funeral* was on the IBBY Honour List and is also translated into German and Spanish.

If you want to contact her to compliment or complain, or read more about her, visit her website: www.paroanand.com. Recently, she gave a TEDx Talk on storytelling.

Wild Child

AND OTHER STORIES

PARO ANAND

PUFFIN BOOKS

PUFFIN BOOKS
Published by the Penguin Group
Penguin Books India Pvt. Ltd, 11 Community Centre, Panchsheel Park, New Delhi 110 017, India
Penguin Group (USA) Inc., 375 Hudson Street, New York, New York 10014, USA
Penguin Group (Canada), 90 Eglinton Avenue East, Suite 700, Toronto, Ontario, M4P 2Y3, Canada (a division of Pearson Penguin Canada Inc.)
Penguin Books Ltd, 80 Strand, London WC2R 0RL, England
Penguin Ireland, 25 St Stephen's Green, Dublin 2, Ireland (a division of Penguin Books Ltd)
Penguin Group (Australia), 250 Camberwell Road, Camberwell, Victoria 3124, Australia (a division of Pearson Australia Group Pty Ltd)
Penguin Group (NZ), 67 Apollo Drive, Rosedale, Auckland 0632, New Zealand (a division of Pearson New Zealand Ltd)
Penguin Group (South Africa) (Pty) Ltd, 24 Sturdee Avenue, Rosebank, Johannesburg 2196, South Africa

Penguin Books Ltd, Registered Offices: 80 Strand, London WC2R 0RL, England

First published in Puffin by Penguin Books India 2011

10 9 8 7 6 5 4 3 2 1

ISBN 9780143332190

The stories 'They Called Her "Fats"' and 'Jason Jamison and I' appeared in *Pepper the Capuchin Monkey and Other Stories* (HarperCollins Publishers India, 1992).

The story 'Eid' appeared as 'After That, in Mumbai' in *Eid Stories* (Scholastic India, 2010)

Typeset in Perpetua by SÜRYA, New Delhi
Printed at Replika Press Pvt. Ltd, Sonepat

To Jaya Bhattacharji Rose for putting up with me at my prima donna worst

And to

Shabir Karam, son and inspiration

Contents

Acknowledgements

TO ALL THE children who have taught me so much and inspired me endlessly, thank you. To organizations such as Vasant Valley School, Bluebells International School, Help Foundation, Rajiv Gandhi Foundation, The World Wide Fund for Nature (WWF) and so many more who ensure that I am always in touch with the reality that surrounds young people.

To Berna and Philo for endless cups of coffee and peace of mind.

And, as always, to Keshav, Aditi and Uday—forever my happiness, my comfort, my compass.

My all.

Wild Child

THERE WAS SOMETHING about this child that was so unappealing. So very odd, really. What was the word for it? Furtive? Yes, that would probably come closest to describing her. If you hauled her up for something she'd done, and oh, she'd always done *something,* she'd stand before you, looking down. As a teacher I always insisted that a child looked at me when I was talking to her. But with Bela, it was impossible. Even when you shouted at her in your '*look at me when I'm talking to you*' big Teacher voice, she'd glance at you for a fleeting instant and then her eyes would dart away, furtively. She definitely had something to hide.

And it wasn't just me who thought that she was a little . . . now, how to put it? A little . . . hmmm . . . I'm trying to think of a kind way of saying it. After all, we teachers are supposed to be kind and understanding. And certainly we're not supposed to condemn little children because of the way they look. Or smell. Yes, she smelt. She had this awful odour around her being. A kind of sour milk smell coupled with really, really bad breath. Her clothes were clean enough, but it was as if she didn't know how to bathe properly. Or brush her teeth. The smell was so bad that sometimes, on the many occasions I had to pull her up, I didn't tell her to look at me when I spoke to her. Because then, if she did open her mouth, I'd be keeling over from the breath of her.

Look, I'm not a bad person. I'm a well-loved teacher, the students love my classes, but there was just something in her that was so un . . . unlikeable. There . . . I've said it. She was unlikeable. And it wasn't just me, she was often the talk of the staff room and there was not one person who had a good thing to say about her. Teachers would come in, flop down at the staff room table and sigh, or tear their hair out, or have a sore throat from yelling at her. Every lesson ended with a barrage of grumbles and complaints about Bela.

And it wasn't just the teachers either. Other students too complained. She was the last to be picked if there was a group activity and if, knowing what was coming, the teacher put her into one of the groups, the other students would openly moan and grumble. And who could blame them? For soon fighting would break out in her group whereas all the others, or at least most of them, would be on their way proceeding with the job at hand. She would spill, break, interrupt and skew the works as only she could. No one wanted to sit next to her. One of my students came up and complained, rather colourfully, 'Ma'm, I can't sit next to her; she smells of last night's puke and pee mixed!' Unkind, but, unfortunately, completely accurate. And then again, it wasn't just the students and teachers. In fact, even parents of other children had sent in complaints, written, telephonic, face-to-face. She stole someone's money or pen, she hit someone, she pushed someone, she wrote on someone else's back, she ate someone else's lunch. Oh, the list was endless! It was as though she did these things only to get caught and get into trouble.

Was it deliberate? Was it that she was expected to behave in a certain way and so she just did? Like, was she just following an expected pattern? I'm no psychologist, but even the school councillor to whom she had been sent umpteen times was unable to improve things for her. Or others. Or find out if there was something bothering her and making her what she was.

To tell you the truth, no one really bothered to find out. We put up with her, knowing that it was probably just for a year and she'd soon be promoted and some other teachers would have the pleasure of dealing with her.

Then, one day, things with Bela spiralled out of control. She got into an awful fight and ripped the shirt off another girl. It was terribly embarrassing for the poor child. The victim, I mean. Weeping, she raced to the bathroom and locked herself in, refusing to come out. At first her friends tried, persuading her that no one had 'seen anything' when her shirt was torn. But this made it even worse for the girl who had probably just started wearing a bra. This was surely a fate worse than death, even. Eventually, after the bell rang and all the children came back to class, I noticed that a bunch of girls was missing.

'Where are the others?' I asked, assuming that they must have been called in for an extra academic class and no one had bothered to inform the mere art teacher that I was. And the whole story came out. Reva had locked herself into the bathroom after having her shirt ripped off. Her friends were trying to persuade her to come out. One had even managed to get a spare tee-shirt for her to put on.

I rushed to the bathroom, eventually got a weeping Reva out and allowed her to go to the sickroom with her best friend to calm down a bit. She did not feel up to facing the others. I came back to a classroom full of enquiries. After all of them settled down, I was about to resume my class when I noticed that Bela was still missing. But no one knew where she was—probably skulking about somewhere. A shudder went down my spine. This was certainly not good. I puzzled over what to do, letting the hum from the class get louder. There were loads of opinions about Bela's disappearance flying about. None of them too good. Teachers were not supposed to leave their classes unattended, but a missing child was a missing child and should be reported to the office immediately. Finally, I made up my mind. I rapped the duster on the desk, sending up a huge cloud of chalk dust, which made me cough.

But, then, I sternly told the children to draw a feeling, whatever feeling they had right now. I said that I would have to go to the office and would be back shortly. I also asked who had seen Bela last. But I think that all the attention had been on Reva and no one thought to see where the attacker was going.

I hesitated just outside the classroom. The decibel level rose immediately as I left. I went back in and gave my class a generous dose of dire warnings. And a last look of appeal. Then I dashed down the corridor, down the steps, across the courtyard to the office. I quickly told the principal's secretary what had happened. I said I was going back to class, because I could already hear shouts of laughter and more coming from that general direction. I said that if I was wanted by the principal, someone needed to be sent to mind the class.

Well, the interim doesn't matter. The details were worked out. The important thing is that Bela was missing. Every sweeper, maali, guard, didi and bhaiya was fanned out around the school compound. Every bathroom, room, storeroom was checked. No Bela. The guard had not seen any child leave the gates. Where could she have gone? It was any school's worst nightmare—to have a child go missing.

There was nothing for it. The parents had to be called. It was the grandparents who came.

Bela's teachers and the principal lined up to meet them. But our aggressive complaints faded as they shuffled into the principal's office, supporting each other, bent over with age and perhaps shame. Or at least embarrassment. Salted over with sorrow, they were just not the kind of young, smart parents who breezed confidently through the school gates. Parents were different now from those from my time, when I was a school girl. For one thing, parents came rarely to school then. They came only when they were called, or rather, hauled, into the principal's office for their child's extra low marks or extra high-handedness. Most times, parents could barely recognize their child's teachers. Now parents came in with sickening regularity. 'Sickening'—for the children, whose lives were pierced and pried into mercilessly, leaving them no privacy. Also sickening for the teachers who became no more than babysitters, forever answerable to the parents for their pupil's shortcomings—as though parenting and genes had nothing to do with it. It was a strictly employer-servant relationship—if the truth be told. So, like the householder could scold the maid for not sweeping behind the sofa, the parent could scold the teacher for not cleaning up the mess that was their child's behaviour or report or whatever. And it was irrelevant who dumped the muck there in the first place.

But I digress. This isn't about how parents treat teachers. It's about how we were going to deal with these grandparents whose arthritic knees prevented them from sitting on the low, soft sofas so that chairs had to be brought in from a classroom. They sat like punished children.

The meeting began, the principal softening the tone she'd come prepared to use. 'Sir, madam,' she began. I didn't envy her. It wasn't going to be easy to tell these old people that we had gone and lost their granddaughter. It may have been entirely her fault, but she was our responsibility. As long as the children were in school, they were ours to look after.

'Sir, madam, we had hoped that Bela's parents would have come.'

'They are not able to come,' the grandfather said.

'We will be taking care of Bela from now on,' the grandmother added softly.

'Is there a change in the child's guardianship, then? We would need to put this into our records if it is the case.'

'It may be so, we will inform you shortly. For the moment, could you tell us what the problem is?'

'Sir, madam,' the principal began again, 'there was a nasty incident this morning.' The old couple exchanged a weary, resigned look. They were used to nasty incidents. As they were told about the shirt tearing, they reacted as though they'd heard this story before. But then, the principal took a deep breath and finally said, 'I am afraid Bela is missing since then. It took us a while to get the information about the incident. By then, some time had elapsed. The guard has strict instructions not to let any child out of the gates unescorted. And he has not seen anyone leave. However, we have thoroughly searched the school campus. And, I am sorry to say that we cannot find her anywhere. We would like to call in the police. We do not know what else to do. We need your permission, your consent to call the police.'

Once again, the grandparents exchanged a look. It was

obvious that this wasn't the first time she had disappeared either.

'May I make a call please,' asked the grandfather. As he took out a little diary from his pocket and carefully dialled the number, the grandmother explained, 'It maybe possible that Bela is in our house. She seeks refuge there when things get too difficult for her.'

'I hope that is the case, madam, but the guard swears that no child has left the school campus.'

'Ah! Our Bela has learnt how to escape when times get too tough. She always finds a way.'

But no, Bela had not found her way to her safe haven this time.

The principal was kneading her temples. The school's owners would be livid with the police being called in. But what else could be done?

The grandparents now suggested that they investigate some places that were her haunts. Places that had served as hideouts before. We glanced at each other. Why did this child need so many hideouts? What was it that she was running from?

I was deputed to drive the grandparents to wherever they needed to go in the hope of finding the missing child. I got my keys and bag and was walking with them towards the car park when a little voice called, 'Nani . . .?'

We looked around. Could it be that she was here all along?

'Bela . . . beta?' her Nani called out, looking around,

not sure where the voice came from, 'Bela, where are you, beta?'

She was on the roof of the school building. Her cropped head peeped over the parapet, four floors up. How had she managed to get up there? The door to the terrace was kept locked. Had she somehow opened it, or found it open?

I rushed the guard up, informing the principal at the same time. The guard found the door secured from the outside. I got a key from the office and made my way up myself. I turned the key in the lock and went to the terrace. She looked like a wild, trapped animal. The whites of her eyes showing as they widened in fear. Her legs braced as though she was ready to spring. Her lips pulled tight over her teeth in a grimace.

'Bela, child, how on earth did you get in here?' I blurted out. To my horror, she pointed at a window that opened up to the staircase. She had used this to get on to the un-railed parapet and then on to the roof where she'd been hiding behind a water tank. No way could we have found her. Thank goodness she'd chosen to reveal herself to her grandparents.

The mixture of relief and anger is a strange cocktail. I was shaking as though I myself had just climbed on to a small parapet four floors up. I put my arms around her. She was as stiff as a log of wood. Unresponsive to my touch. In fact, I think she flinched. 'Bela, Bela, you could have fallen, do you know what a dangerous thing you've done?'

'No, Ma'm, it's okay, I don't fall,' she replied, shaking me off. So she had done this before. And none of us knew. No one had missed her when she'd disappeared before.

She ran to her grandmother once we'd come down. She sobbed and cried and begged to go home. But in the meantime, the principal had received a call from Reva's parents who had called to tell them about how she'd been attacked.

'We don't want wild animals in our children's classroom,' they'd said. They insisted that punitive action be taken. 'Or else we will have to take up the matter with Higher Authorities.' They'd said.

Once it is opened, it is impossible to shut a can of worms. And so they came crawling out until the ugly truth lay like a menacing, writhing thing in front of us. Bela sat kicking a chair in the adjoining room. We could hear her 'whack, whack, whack, whack . . .'

The grandparents told us the truth about their grandchild. Bela's troubles had begun at home, where she lived with a very violent father. One day, he had beaten his wife to the point of senselessness. And then he'd turned on Bela, trying to molest her. But she screamed and shouted till her mother dragged herself back to consciousness. Seeing the father abusing the child, Bela's mother had picked up a pressure cooker full of dal and she had hit her husband over the head with it. Smashing it down on to his skull.

He had gone down like a squashed fly. Right on top of his

daughter who sobbed, too frightened to speak. The police had come and taken the father's body away. And then they'd taken Bela's mother—to prison. She was awaiting her trial.

When the grandparents finished narrating the horrific incidents, we were all shaken, trembling with the enormity of what we'd heard. Ashamed, almost, that we'd just treated Bela like a wild child who needed disciplining. Never once wondering what had happened to her in her young, little life.

There was no way that we could send her away now. Reva's parents would have to understand. We would have to work on the other children too, to ensure that they were not isolating this child any longer. I knew, we all knew it was going to be an uphill task, but we also knew that we'd been given a chance to make one life just a little, little bit better.

We would get there.

This is Shabir Karam . . .

by Shabir Karam and Paro

'MY NAME IS Shabir Karam,' said the boy in a voice that was so soft, it was barely audible. But no one asked him to speak any louder, for most of the other children gathered there also spoke in voices that were soft. Not shy soft, but scared soft—the hesitation more audible than the words themselves. No one could see his eyes either, for they were well protected under the peaked cap, worn low over his brow, concealing who knew what grief in those deep brown eyes. The shoulders drooped over, as though carrying a burdensome weight. And indeed, there was a weight. The weight of knowledge greater than a fourteen year old should have. More experience than a young life should bear.

He barely heard the names of the others,except when the sharp voice of a young girl rang out with more aggressive confidence than any other voice in the room. 'Hum inkey naam nahin yaad kar saktey. Sorry, sir, but no way can we remember these people's names. They are too different from ours!' Shabir looked up and was frightened by the rage in those grey eyes that spoke out so vehemently.

Shabir couldn't help the shudder of sudden resentment that shot through him. He looked up at her, glancing around, relieved that everyone was looking at the girl and no one looked at him. He hated to be noticed at all. The girl sat straight-backed, her chin thrust out in defiance. What was she so resentful about? Shabir wondered. After all, she was a Hindu and the Hindus had just taken the coward's way out. They had upped and left the Kashmir valley when the trouble started getting really bad. When the militants came and shot families and robbed food and forced girls to go with them. The Hindus left the valley and fled to safety, leaving the Muslims to hold the fort themselves. All right, the Hindus had left their homes, their fields, their jobs and businesses. But at least the Hindus were safe now. They were no longer living under curfews and stone pelting and bomb explosions.

Yet this girl had the nerve to sit there, so straight-backed and fire-eyed and say that she and her friends refused to try and remember Muslim names. This was the first time he'd met a Hindu. He knew that all the children gathered here had lost their fathers to militancy. Muslims and Hindus, both. But the stories that he'd always heard about Hindus seemed to be true. They were a resentful lot, never satisfied, always thrusting their own troubles on to Muslims, blaming them for all the ills they suffered. Everybody here had suffered, so what was she so resentful about?

It was a boy sitting opposite Shabir who voiced his thoughts, 'Well, we can't remember *their* names either,' he smirked, 'after all, these Hindu names are different for us.'

The battle lines were drawn. Shabir cast his eyes down again and sighed. There could never be peace between Hindus and Muslims. Why were these people of the NGO that was supporting the orphans of militancy in Kashmir intent on putting the two communities together? What were they hoping to achieve? There could never be peace between them. There could never be peace in the valley. It was no longer the famed paradise on earth. And never would be again. Shabir felt the hopelessness engulf him once more.

But soon it was his turn. Shabir's heart sank. They were playing this silly game that the NGO aunties were making them play. All the children were sitting in a circle and had to say the names of everyone sitting there. How was it possible? There were days when Shabir could barely remember his own name. Days when silence wrapped him in such a dense fog that he heard nothing, noticed nothing. The fog was closing in on him again now.

And as always, the fog drew him back into the black hole that was the day when his life changed forever.

He was a little boy then, clinging on to his mother's hand. Running to keep alongside her as she pulled him along, food for her husband hanging in a basket in her other hand. His father sold cloth for cloth shops. He'd wheel his barrow to local markets and set up his stall wherever the pickings seemed promising. He was a devout man, saying his prayers five times a day. And he was a loving father to his daughters. But his favourite was his youngest. His little son—whom he had named Shabir Karam.

Shabir loved to sit in his father's lap and listen to stories about his father's day. His father would tell him all kinds of tales about the customers who came to his stall that day. The cloth they were looking for. Gauzy prints and silky lengths. Beautiful cloths. Coarse cloths. Oh, all kinds of cloth to stitch into fancy clothes. But best of all, Shabir loved the stories that his father told about the special, fantastical creatures that came to examine his wares. Shabir would stare wide-eyed, his imagination racing, as in his mind's eye he conjured up the images of these strange monsterly creatures. There were always a few of these who came to visit his father, along with the other normal human beings. His father's wild imagination embellished his creatures with elephants' trunks and roses growing in places of hair.

He always hurried along his mother's side as they went to deliver food to him. He always hoped to catch a glimpse of one these creatures at his father's stall. But, till now, his father always laughed and said that they had left just moments before he arrived.

As he raced along his mother's side, Shabir recalled how he had once begged his father to capture one of the magical creatures and bind it with a strong rope and keep it there till Shabir arrived. But his Abbu jaan had admonished him gently and said that it would be cruel to be so rough with his precious customers. That's what he loved most about his father. He was kind, even to strange creatures and monsters . . .

Shabir was drawn back into the present by the repeated nudging in his side. He looked up, startled to see several pairs of eyes on him. One of the NGO aunties nodded at him, 'Come Shabir, it's your turn now, you have to say the names of all the children here. Come, I'll help you with it,' and she started to take the names one by one. Shabir dully repeated the names after her, not really taking in any of them. Especially not the Hindu names that tasted strange on his tongue.

He was still in his world of awful memories. Although his mind struggled against those recurrent waking dreams, although his heart cried out that he could not bear to see the scene of his long ago childhood again, he was irrevocably drawn back into the nightmare.

His father stands. Tall. Proud. He is holding a length of bright green cloth. A customer leans forward, fingers it. He is dressed in an over-sized dark black phiran. At last. At last. Has the child reached in time? At last! Perhaps this customer is one of the monsters. He tugs, tugs, tugs his mother forward. Hurry, hurry, he urges. Leaning forward. He starts to run as the monster puts his hand into a bag he carries. A big, black bag. 'Ammi,' the child screams, 'Ammi hurry!' he runs forward. But then . . .

But then suddenly he is thrown back, back, back—back into deathly deafening blackness. The fog wrapping him in its filthy embrace. Cries. Shrieks. He hears his mother—wailing, wailing,

wailing. Hiding behind her, peeping out, he searches for his father. Abbu? . . . he wants to tell him to stop Ammi's tears. But his Abbu jaan's cart is no longer where it had stood just moments ago. All he can see is a shred of his father's phiran. There's nothing more left of him now. Nothing left.

Shabir now fingers the shred of his father's phiran. The little scrap that he keeps in his pocket. Always. He knows now that the man standing fingering the green cloth so long ago was indeed a monster. A monster in the shape of a suicide bomber. He wishes now, as he has a thousand times before, that his father had indeed taken his instruction and tied the monster up with a strong rope. Then maybe, just maybe, Abbu jaan would have been alive today.

The repetition of names is almost over. The fire-eyed girl looks at him with a mixture of curiosity and what is it? Sympathy? When it is her turn, she repeats the names with some help from the organizers of the camp. But when she comes to his name, she smiles at him and says—Shabir. He likes the sound of his name on her tongue. She emphasizes the 'b' as though it were a double 'bb' sound. He lands back into the present with a smile at her. He is pleased that she remembered his name without help. She narrows her eyes at him then raises her eyebrows. She's asking him a question, but he doesn't know how to answer. He shrugs his shoulders and gives his head a slight shake.

Then he forces himself to concentrate on what the women conducting the session are saying. And he is strangely surprised at what they are saying. Strange because he did know it all along, yet strange, because he had never thought of it before. They're talking about the bond that binds them all here. The thread that ties them. Their losses. The deaths that they have witnessed in their families. All the children here have witnessed loss. Shabir had never thought of it before. He is not the only one who lost his father. There are many. All the children here. The Muslims and the Hindus. They've all lost. They are all lost.

He looks again at the girl.

He's never met a Hindu before, but she seems nice. Even though she seems full of fire, she has a nice smile. He gives her a small wave from across the room. She turns away, but not before he sees a smile break the seriousness of her face.

He's never met a Hindu before, but maybe he is the first Muslim she's met. And maybe, just maybe, they can be friends. After all.

~

(This story is inspired by a young man, my son, Shabir Karam with whom I have worked in Srinagar through the Rajiv Gandhi Foundation. I hope he can live well to fight the monsters that lurk in our paradise.)

They Called Her 'Fats'

THEY CALLED HER 'Fats', although her name was Fatima. And she wasn't even fat. At least, not in that nice, pudgy way that makes little girls look adorable to adults. She wasn't adorable or sweet, or anything like the sugar and spice and everything nice that little girls are supposedly made of. In fact, she was BAD. Bad in big, bold, capital letters. She was a fighter and had been so ever since she came to the Home as a four-year-old orphan. She'd been in another home before that. She'd been left there, at the doorstep—abandoned by the mother no one would ever know. That orphanage looked after infants. Now, at four, she was considered old enough to move to a new environment. She'd never been adopted as some of the other babies had.

She hated the new Home from her first day there. She perceived a greyness that filled her with dismay. The forced cheerfulness of the care-mothers and nurses turned to bile inside her and they soon became wary of her sullen, brooding eyes. Never knowing when she'd snap back at them. They kept as much out of the way of this tiny, less than lovely child as they could.

She wasn't much better with her peers either. The girls returned her sullenness with hostility. In fact, they sniggered behind her back and kept their eyes averted when they came face-to-face with her. Fatima concluded it was because they feared her obvious unhappiness. As though it were a contagious disease they were afraid they'd catch. They wore their happiness like badges. Fatima wore her grief like armour. And there was no one who cared to find the chinks in that formidable armour to reach the inner depths that must have lurked in this unhappy child.

And the boys—the boys. They laughed at her openly. It was the boys, in fact, who coined the nickname 'Fats'. They referred to it like a Mafia underworld underling. Like 'Bugs' or 'Lefty'.

They spread malicious stories about her which were mean and untrue. Of how she communed with the spirits of darkness in the middle of the night, of her witchery and her penchant for drinking blood and eating cockroaches off the floor. Stories that made the girls squeal with appealing girlish charm and cling on to the boys' arms in prettily feigned terror. Some were masters in the art of swooning into convenient arms and could only be revived by the undivided attention of a male admirer.

It made Fatima sick to her stomach. But she also did everything she could to fuel the stories. She dangled cockroaches by their writhing legs and threw them at the screaming girls. She left her dormitory late at night in spite of repeated warnings from the house warden.

What she did outside on the dew-damp lawns of the sports field was nothing more bloodthirsty than walk barefoot on the wet grass and rest her head on the cool moss-covered stone walls. For she loved her solitude and guarded it like her most precious treasure. Some nights, she would slip, ghostlike on to the games field and jog around the track. Bursting now and then into a spirited sprint. She loved the feel of the wind as it whipped past her ears and stung her cheeks. It was about the only time in that place that Fatima allowed herself to laugh out aloud. In a sudden rush of warmth that she dared not describe as happiness, she would leap into the air, arms flailing, and whoop with joy.

But then, one night, a couple of girls from her ward followed her stealthily and watched her strange ritual from behind a bush.

The story spread like wildfire. Fats indulged in some sort of witch's dance—calling spirits and dancing, prancing with them on the games field. And now there were two reliable witnesses to this bizarre ritual to prove the fact, which they did; gladly and frequently. Word soon reached the hostel warden.

The warden looked at the down-turned dark head. There was no grace, no flicker of softness, no feminine charm to this child. The warden thought as she drummed her fingertips together, not quite sure how to tackle this problem twelve year old. Being in charge of a host of orphans was not the easiest of jobs, but never, in all her years here, had the warden had to handle such a bad apple as Fatima had been termed by the orphanage authorities.

'I'm afraid, Fatima, I have been hearing stories about you,' the warden began. Fatima lifted her head to look steadily just past the warden's right ear, as though staring at a spider that hung there. Knowing she shouldn't, the older woman turned her head to check. No, there was no spider, or anything else. There wasn't, of course not. When she looked back at the girl's face, she was embarrassed by the brief look of triumph that flickered there.

'I need some explanations from you, my child.'

'I'm NOT your child!' screamed Fatima in her head. But she kept her gaze steady and unflinching on the spot just past the warden's ear. The woman rubbed her ear self-consciously, as though cooling it from that burning gaze.

'What exactly were you doing, young lady, out on the games field in the middle of the night?'

A million answers raced through her mind. Some witty, some smart, some downright rude. But 'running' was all she said.

'And why, my dear, do you choose to run in the middle of the night? Don't you find the games period enough?'

'No!'

The warden pursed her lips in astonishment at the abrupt, instant reply. She gathered herself up, 'And why, may I ask, do you feel it's not enough?'

No reply. Fatima just stared steadily at the spot beyond that right ear.

'Hmmm?' asked the warden, again involuntarily glancing over her shoulder to ascertain what it was that this unsettling girl was staring at.

Answers whirled through Fatima's head. A part of her wanted to tell of her love for running. How it was the only time she felt free. Really, really free. She wanted to tell of her love for true solitude. She wanted, so desperately needed, to tell of the pain she felt when the girls sniggered, at the humiliation of them whispering, 'Shhh! Here comes Fats to bite your tongue out!' Of the boys who taunted her of being a half-boy, half-girl. She had so much boiling up inside her.

But she stood her ground. She held her silence—biting back her words of hurt. Fighting back the tears that threatened to break loose and show the world that she was, after all, human.

Instead, she stood still and silent. Over the years, she had trained herself to speak only when spoken to, and then only in uncommunicative monosyllables that discouraged conversation. She gave nothing of herself away, maintaining a stony calm on the outside while her emotions raged inside her.

'Well, if you're not going to answer, there's very little I can do to help you, is there?' asked the cold voice.

'*There's very little you can do anyway . . .*' thought Fatima, biting back the words in the nick of time. A twitching in the jaw was the only indication that this was a living girl and not a cold waxwork that stood so stone-faced and still.

'Very well, then,' the warden stood up, pulling self-consciously at her ear, 'if that's the attitude, you may go . . .' Fatima turned on her heel immediately. '. . . but let me warn you, young lady. I do not tolerate my rules being broken. If I have any more complaints against you, I shall have to suspend your games outings altogether. Is that clear?' Sometimes the only way to discipline a wayward ward was to threaten to withdraw a favourite privilege.

'Yes Ma'am!' the voice was so quiet, so cold, that it sent an involuntary shiver down the warden's back.

'You may go.'

Fatima strode to the door and opened it when a softening in the warden's voice drew her up short.

'If, however, you need to talk to me about anything, er, anything at all, you're always welcome to come to me. Any time at all, all right?'

Fatima nodded, hesitated and looked back at the older woman. It was almost as if she was about to say something. But then, she quickly stepped out and shut the door firmly behind her, hurrying away—burying her words and feelings yet again.

The warden looked out through her window. Fatima passed along the periphery of the field. A group of children laughed pointedly at the solitary figure as it slipped away and was soon lost amongst the bushes. The warden knew the interview had not gone at all well. She wished she could do more for this closed, closed child. But she just didn't know where to start. How to open the first window to her heart and mind?

Now that her nightly ritual had been forcibly brought to a halt, Fatima just had to make the most of the allotted games periods. She had never allowed herself to participate wholeheartedly and now she stood on the outskirts of the action, watching her classmates through brooding eyes, wondering which game she should join. And more important and infinitely more difficult was, *how* she would join it.

'Watch out, stupid!' A scream broke into her thoughts. Suddenly she was conscious of people screaming at her. A flash of silver whistled past her face and she watched in shocked amazement as the wooden pole slithered to a halt just beyond her. Almost in a trance, she bent down and picked up the pole and gingerly fingered the sharply pointed end.

'Are you all right? You're not hurt, are you?' Mrs Whitbread, the games teacher grabbed the girl by the shoulders and turned her around.

'No, no . . .' Fatima stuttered, still holding on to the pole.

'What an idiot you are Fats,' hissed a girl into her ear, 'what were you thinking of, witches?'

'Hush, quiet, it wasn't her fault,' Mrs Whitbread quietened the other as she led Fatima away, arm still around her shoulders.

'You should not stand here. If you want to watch, stand

across there, at that corner. Here now, let me have the javelin . . .' but the teacher was surprised as the silent girl held on to it, in a grip so tight that her knuckles had turned white. And she didn't let it go. They stood like that a full, silent minute, both holding the spiked instrument. Then the girl abruptly released it as though it had become red hot.

'Sorry,' she said as she walked rapidly away. Something in the girl's silence, something in her lingering hold over the javelin, kept Mrs Whitbread rooted to the spot, looking at the girl's retreating back.

During the next day's class, Mrs Whitbread had the absurd feeling that someone was staring at her. Hard. From the corner of her eye, she caught sight of the slight frame which stood stock-still. Staring. It was Fatima. Margaret Whitbread called out and waved her over, but the girl was gone, speeding away like a frightened rabbit. It happened again, the next two classes. Then on the third day, just when the games teacher had expected to see her standing at her usual corner, she was surprised that Fatima was nowhere in sight. Mrs Whitbread shrugged off the terrible feeling of disappointment that was stealing over her and got back into training the children around her. Being a former British international javelin thrower herself, she gave a lot of personal attention to that sport although she was the general sports in charge.

Just as she became absorbed in a promising young boy, a voice from behind startled her.

'All right, I'll join for javelin!' short, abrupt, to the point. She wasn't seeking permission—just stating her acquiescence. It was, of course, Fatima. In spite of the abruptness of the pronouncement, the teacher could not suppress a smile.

And so it was that Fatima began to learn to throw the javelin.

An hour later, it was the talk of the staff room.

'Oh, poor you!' was the general consensus of all the teachers when Margaret Whitbread announced this new development. 'Poor you, now you've had it.'

'I don't know,' she answered, 'maybe. But then again, maybe not . . .'

'Oh, that girl is nothing but trouble.'

'She's the most disruptive child anyone's ever had the misfortune to deal with.'

'True,' agreed Margaret, 'but there's no getting away from the fact that this is the first positive move the child has made in all her stay here. The first time she's shown an interest in doing something.'

'Oh, don't waste your optimism on her; there are better candidates for that.'

'I'm going to give it a shot,' Margaret insisted.

'Well, best of luck is all I'd care to say to you, love,' said a teacher laughing.

'Right,' agreed another, 'I wouldn't care to be in your shoes. Not for all the money in the world . . .'

Even the children were only too willing to consider the turn of events in the darkest possible way.

'It's all a part of her secret rituals, you know—throwing the lance, spearing unsuspecting victims.'

'Of all the sports there are, isn't it strange that she chose the most medieval of them all?' they sniggered.

But Fatima turned her back on the gossip as she showed up for the first practice session. Mrs Whitbread straightaway noticed the fierce concentration with which the girl applied herself. Her eyebrows knitted together, her jaw pulsing, she looked and listened with keen interest as the teacher taught her how to grip the javelin, how to support it on her finger, how to balance her body before the run up. How to brace herself for the throw.

The grip. The run. The leaning back and then—the throw. Fatima hopped on one leg, arm extended for balance and a thrill shot through her as the javelin soared, zinging through the air. And landed with a perfect TCHACK! Steel tip buried snugly in the earth—pole vibrating with energy.

She spun around, eyes shining. The teacher nodded, eyes shining too. It was good. Not very far, but it was a great first throw. Neat and true. The technique was right. It was an auspicious start, full of promise, certainly better than Mrs Whitbread had seen a first timer throw before.

Each child was given three throws before handing over the javelin to the next one. Then they waited for their turn to come around once again. Fatima could barely contain her impatience. She waited for her turn, almost hopping from one foot to the other. It had been years, perhaps all her life that she had felt eager to do something, motivated to achieve. She didn't notice it then, but the others did. It was also the first time that she allowed her eagerness to show, or at least, she didn't struggle to bury it.

Her hand shook in eager anticipation as she gripped the lance again. She shut her eyes momentarily, gathering her strength, reining in her thoughts. It did feel like she was taking part in a ritual. There was something mythical in the spear. When she started her run, the javelin became an integral part of her and when it flew, eagle-light, from her hand, it was as if her soul went with it. Guiding it with soaring spirit, ripping through the air, reaching for the sky. Before starting its descent. It was the longest throw that had ever been recorded in the school.

'Witchcraft . . .' mumbled the boy who'd had his turn before hers. Thrice his javelin had fouled, landing flat, skidding over the grass like a wounded snake, instead of the satisfying sound of the tip biting into the earth.

Fatima heard his words. She bit down on her tongue to stop the retaliation that was in her throat. The hurt turned to acid in her stomach.

She began her run for the third time, this time without the mental preparation, without the ritual. As she released the spear, a muscle jarred through her shoulder like an electric shock. She didn't need to look to know that the throw was no good. No comforting *Tchack* accompanied the landing of the javelin into the ground. It was a flat throw.

The same boy sniggered as she passed him. And, almost against her will, she lost control. Balling her hand into a fist, she flung a punch at him. He was down on the ground in an instant. The teacher was beside her, taking hold of her shoulders, pushing her gently, firmly away.

'No, Fatima, that's enough now. Stop it. I said, stop it!'

'I'm *sick* of it,' the girl hissed with so much venom that Mrs Whitbread was taken aback.

'Get him to the nurse's room, inform his house warden.' The teacher instructed some of the other students as she held on to Fatima. The boy was not badly hurt, just winded, really.

'Sick! Sick! Sick! Sick! Sick!!!!' spat the girl.

'Hush now, shh, quiet, quiet . . .' soothed the teacher, hurrying Fatima away now. Fatima's face was flushed, her eyes blazing with rage. The heat of anger emanated from her as she allowed herself to be led away.

But as they approached the empty common room, the girl baulked.

'No! Don't bring me here to sweet-talk me. I'm not interested. I don't need your lip sympathy or moral lectures on being a good girl. I don't need any confidantes, okay? Just leave me alone. I don't need anyone. Anything! Ever!'

She struggled to be free, but the teacher still held her with strong hands. 'I'm not here to sweet-talk anybody. I don't give out sympathy for free either. But I do think we ought to talk.' Her voice was firm, no nonsense. Fatima was forced to listen as she continued, 'Look, Fatima, you're too good at javelin; I can see it in just one morning. You're too good to just throw it all away because someone made some stupid, irrelevant remark.' She saw she had the girl's attention. She let go of her shoulders.

'Now, I'm going into the common room and I'll wait five minutes. If you think we can talk like sensible human beings, you can come right in. If not . . .' she shrugged, leaving her sentence hanging in mid-air.

She went into the empty room and shut the door behind her. Here she closed her eyes and ran a hand over her face. She was surprised to find that her head hurt. She wanted so much to be able to open the door to this child's mind and let some fresh air in. She had so much promise, but was also ever ready to press the self-destruct button in panic. Was there something that she, as a teacher, an older woman, a mother, could do?

The door opened, creaking, unwillingly, just a crack. The teacher couldn't see for sure who it was.

'Come on in, Fatima,' she said in a voice that exuded more confidence than she felt. And then she was there. Standing there, glowering.

'Well?' she demanded, standing in the open doorway, arms akimbo, 'what is it that we need to talk about?'

'Why don't you shut the door and come sit down?' the teacher said.

But the girl shook her head, holding the door ajar, ready to bolt, 'no, there's no need. This isn't going to take long.'

'As you like. Fatima, I was wondering, would you like to take special javelin lessons? Say in the evenings?'

'Why?'

The older woman smiled, 'Why—what?'

'Why should I want *special* sessions?' Fatima said as though 'special' was a dirty, forbidden word.

'Well, two reasons, I think. One, I believe you could be very good at it.'

'And number two?'

Margaret suppressed her smile; there was something so sweet in Fatima's belligerence.

'For reasons best known to yourself, Fatima, you don't seem to get on with the other children. Anyway, that's not my concern, really, but maybe you'd prefer to practice on your own, er, with me, of course, if you don't mind . . .' and she laughed out aloud. She saw the brief look of pleasure that flickered across the child's face, although she was silent.

'All right, that's settled then. I'll meet you this evening at five.' The teacher was almost out of the door before she heard it.

'Thank you,' a tiny voice. Mrs Whitbread turned and smiled a little smile in silent acknowledgement—perhaps of a new bond.

Later that night, at home with her husband and sons, Mrs Whitbread talked of young Fatima. It was one of the few times that she discussed the orphanage children with her family. They too now sensed that it was with special feeling that she spoke of this girl. And they were to hear a lot more of her.

Fatima trained hard under her mentor's tutelage. She never complained of being tired. She never lost focus or enthusiasm. Day by day, Mrs Whitbread came to realize that she had a very special athlete in her care.

'You know, Fatima,' said Mrs Whitbread one evening as they wiped the sweat of their hour of weight training off their faces. 'In many countries, you wouldn't even have been allowed to train for javelin.'

'Why not, what's wrong with me?'

'Your height, you know. You're just five feet four inches tall. And if you ever get to compete at an international level, you'll be at a disadvantage against your opponents who'd be inevitably taller and stronger.'

Fatima listened, then silently considered. Then she straightened up and said, 'I *will* compete at international levels, Mrs Whitbread. I may not be tall, but I'll make myself stronger, and I'll beat the competition!' The twitching of that determined jawline fired the teacher's imagination and she thought that it might well be so.

Margaret obtained special permission from the teachers and warden who were all secretly, even overtly, relieved to have less of this child to deal with. The games teacher also requested her own family's indulgence for her frequent absences and late nights. Seeing how charged up with enthusiasm she was, they didn't have the heart to refuse her.

Fatima's training became more intense and rigorous. What she lacked in height had to be made up in sheer power, and that meant building up the right muscles in the right places. The results soon became apparent. As she packed more power behind each throw, the javelin sliced through the air further and further. And now Fatima didn't bother to hide her exultation.

The jibes and comments still came sporadically. Some girls passed comments that she was turning into a boy, the way her arms rippled with muscles. But they didn't bother Fatima at all now. She was proud of her muscles. They were won after a lot of sweat and païn and effort. Gradually, seeing her go from one success to another, the comments turned to grudging admiration.

From a passing fancy now, the mystical javelin became an obsession with Fatima, now fourteen and bulging with biceps.

And Fatima too became an obsession with her games teacher. They would train two or three times a day and sometimes the girl would pack in an extra session by herself. She had learned, with her mentor's help, not to let anyone's comments about her, or her unfeminine appearance, bother her. She loved the javelin and for that she needed those muscles. She wore them like a badge of honour.

One night, when Mrs Whitbread couldn't keep the excitement from her voice about Fatima's unparalleled talent and her love for her, one of her sons suggested, 'Why don't we adopt her, Mom? You love her so much!' said he with so much conviction, not malice. The older woman smiled and looked at the rest of her family.

And so it happened. Fatima, the problem child, the disruptive influence, at the age of fourteen, finally got what most of us are born with, what we take for granted. At the age of fourteen, Fatima finally got a family and a surname to call her own.

And she went on to live up to that name and make her new-found family proud to have her in their midst.

~

Fatima Whitbread went on to win an Olympic bronze medal and later, in 1986, the World Championship, making five of the six longest throws in history and shattering the world record. Said she, 'I stood on the victory stand and listened while they played my national anthem. I was tired and my arm ached, (from injections needed for an ailment she suffered from), but I had never felt better in my life!'

Long ago, a little news item on the sports page of a newspaper told me something of this incredible woman. Since then, I have tried to gather as much information about her as possible. The basic facts of this story are true, with some embellishments and additions to make the fabric of this bio-fiction. Let's say, it's conjecture in good faith.

Fatima Whitbread, we salute you.

Santa's Not So Little Helper

I AM SO, so utterly mad at my dad. He's gone and hurt his back. Just when he'd promised we'd go on one of those dad-son bonding camping trips—like they do in movies. But no, he HAD to go and lift furniture for mom. It's like they were doing this on purpose. It was going to be such a great, great trip. Camping, fishing, cooking food over a bonfire—the works! Plus, no mum to nag. And the best part of all of it was that I was going to miss a week of school. Dad had got special permission from the head and all. I was going to miss the essay writing test too, which was just too cool. I hate essay writing. I mean, what's the point of it? I can never quite figure.

And then, mom made dad move furniture. I mean, what's the need to disturb dust that's been lying quietly behind the beds and sofas? It's not bothering anyone. No one can see it. Leave it. But NO . . . cleaning hidden dust balls was more important than father-son bonding time. So I'm back to sitting in class, a week before the winter vacation, resentful as hell. And as if that wasn't bad enough, the teacher says that we're going to have the essay writing test today, instead of two days later. That just sucks. Because I was going to blackmail mom into writing it for me and just mugging it up. I hate these surprises. It had been a week of unpleasant shocks for me. I should look at the horoscope and check. I'm sure there's some star freaking up my present and future. A 'horrorscope' most likely.

Anyway, now there's no way out, we've got to write our essay. Then the teacher puts the topic up on the board. Christmas! I mean, are you serious? Christmas? That's like for four year olds. Please, why can't grown-ups get clued on to the fact that fourteen year olds do NOT write essays about Christmas cheer and Christmas spirit. I mean, seriously? We all let out collective moans and protests. But this Mrs Pimply-faced Pandey is immune to us. We call her Pimply Panda because she's got pimples (duh!) even though she's a grown-up, married woman—I mean, disgusting! And she's got dark circles around her eyes, panda-like. Like she's got the worst of youth and old age, all on her face. Poor thing. Not that I'm feeling in the least bit sympathetic towards her right now, as she ignores our howls of protests and tells us that we've just got thirty minutes left, so we'd best get going. Then she tries to cheer us up by telling us that she's got a special prize for the winner. Yeah, a toffee or something, I bet. I mean, I wouldn't want to be the idiot who wins an essay writing competition on the topic Christmas. I mean, poor sucker, he'll be the butt of jokes for the rest of his life! I shudder and start chewing the much chewed end of my ball pen, wondering what to write about. Then I thought about Santa. What kind of dad was he? Did his kids like him as much as the rest of the world loves Santa? Or did they resent him at times, the way we kids resent our dads? Hmm . . .

Santa's Not So Little Helper
by
Gautam (9C)

So, like it's that time of the year again. And like I've been doing this thing for so long, but my old man, he like, keeps telling me to pull up my socks —yeah, soCKS with a 'c' and a 'k', no 'sox' for my dad. No sir. That's one C and K he likes, not the other one, which I like to use, if you know what I mean. He's a serious kind of dude, although, you know, no one thinks of Santa as being serious. According to the world he's the old 'Ho Ho Ho' kind-of-guy. But no one thinks to ask us. Like his kids. He's not so Ho Ho with us. He keeps us on a strict leash. Almost. So, dad keeps yelling at me, pull your soCKS up. Any time he sees me relaxing. And like its not as if I've even got any sox (hah!) to pull up. Like what's with these weird green tights or leggings we're supposed to wear? I mean, it was one thing when we were like, eight—but boy, at fourteen, its kind of whack, right?

Anyways, I've been working with my old man since I was eight or something. I mean talk about child labour dude —my old man never seems to get in trouble with the dudes, you know who I mean—those cop guys? Like, we don't even get paid or anything, y' know. It's supposed to be cool if you don't pay the kids—and that's like totally weird to me, man. I mean, why's it not child labour if the child's not paid? We're children and what we do sure feels like labour, you know? Not that I want my dad to be in trouble with the law or anything. It's just that it's a lot of hard work you know? And I wouldn't mind getting paid and stuff. I asked my dad once, like I told him he should pay me and stuff. He blew a huge fuse. As if it was murder. And even mom was mad at me for saying this. She tried to guilt-trip me saying that I should love what I do and do it for the honour and stuff. But I don't have a guilty bone in my body. I don't feel it, man.

So, anyway, getting back to the point. We read the wish lists, and then we make the toys, wrap them, pack them, label them, address them. And if all that's not enough, we then got to deliver them. And we're not as lucky as those pizza guys either, who get like fat tips and stuff for every pizza they drop off at your house. We? We get squat. And no off days either, at least not when it's THAT TIME OF THE YEAR!!!

Now I guess y'all are wondering what I'm on

about? Truth be told, though, at fourteen, I'm truly ashamed to say this—I'm Santa's not so little helper!

It's truly weird man, we do all this work and then there are you guys out there who don't even believe in us! How can you not believe I exist? It's like I don't believe you exist—you'd find that sorta freaky, wouldn't you? You're there, you do all this stuff, and then along comes some freak who says 'Sorry, I don't believe in you, or your old man.' So then, how'd you get all those presents—Huh? I mean, d'you really believe that your old man, whose been a tight wad all 364 days in the year, suddenly wakes up one fine day and decides ok, today I'll get my darling baby the X-Box, the MP3 player, the Shuffle iPod, the soccer gear, the blue tooth or blue jeans, the expensive sweater, the sleek laptop backpack or whatever it is that your heart desires? You've GOT to be joking. I mean, surely that's harder to believe than good old Santa. What's he ever done to make you think, like ok, this guy doesn't exist—he's worse than a dinosaur, because they at least existed, this guy does not. Never did. Well, I've got news for you pal. He does. We do. There is a Santa and I'm his son, his little helper. And you've got your Bluetooth to prove it.

I mean, sure I can understand that it's hard for you to get that there's this freakishly old man who has nothing better to do than spend a year making stuff for you and then giving it away and then not even coming by for a thank you, let alone a payment. Yeah, it is weird, come to think of it. I think I'd, like, flip a fish about it too. But, well, there was a time when my mom would be whining about it, telling him he had to stop giving away stuff that she had good use for. Like there was this laptop that had all her poetry and stuff that she was writing. She was planning to get it published and all. Said she was sick of just being Mrs Santa who no one ever thinks about. Like there are no Mrs Santa carols and stuff. Anyway, so there was all her poetry on this laptop. And then, whoosh, the whole laptop's gone—given to some whiny guy who had it down on his wish list. That was the year when lots of kids wanted those. There are these trends— suddenly, there's something that everybody wants. Needs. That year, it was laptops. We were making them for months, but then we were one piece short, so my dear dad just picks up the one at home and ships it off to some nerdy needy guy in India, or somewhere! Boy did my dad get into trouble for that! We didn't get any Christmas dinner that night. And we don't even have any pizza delivery here, because the pizza guys or the other takeaways don't believe in us. Freaky . . .

Anyway, like now I've been put into the assembly line wrapping and sorting stuff into where it has to go. I'm next to this awful guy. I hate him—he's a cousin of some sort, I've never figured what exactly. He's a pimply-faced nerd—ok, I'm pretty pimply-faced myself, but I'm fourteen, what'd you expect? This cousin guy, though, he's some ten or something and he's already got the grossest pimples, you know, the two fried eggs kind? And he's got these really thick glasses, he looks at you and it's like you're looking through the bottom of a coke bottle or something. You'd think he'd ask good old Santa for better eyes—yeah, yeah, I know, Santa doesn't go around distributing body parts. I know that, but contact lenses, at least? But that's the other thing. We don't get to give Santa our wish lists. We're supposed to get all our joy making and giving away stuff. Bleah!

Anyway, I really hate this guy. I know we're not supposed to, like, hate anyone around here. Hate and greed are two big no-nos in Santa land. But that's just too weird for me. How is anybody supposed to like everybody? My dad and mom say like, I've got bad attitude and that I think I'm awfully superior, but I'm not. But, I can tell you one thing, I am superior to this guy, no doubt about it. I really hate him. Not for his pimples or eyes or anything, but because he grosses me out with his nose picking. His nostrils have become like, craters of a volcano, with all that picking. He could wrap his presents in all that . . . ugh!

Right now, he's gross and close and chatting to me about how he's so excited that he's going on his first delivery round. Yeah, he's happy now, wait till he's out there in the cold. Sleepy and confused, trying to get into houses that have these fancy alarm systems. And no hot drink or even a thank you note left out for us. I wonder if I was as excited as he is. I don't think so, I was never, like, so excited about anything. He's planning on going with Santa himself.

Not on the sleigh or anything. We don't use the flying reindeer any more. The animal rights people started objecting about it. Too bad, really, that was the best part of the whole deal. But they said that we were abusing the animals by making them fly and that too at night, away from their natural habitat and stuff. The reindeer were pretty sad about it. Old Rudolf's nose went really pale and almost stopped glowing altogether. That was until he met this really cool chick reindeer with a blue nose though it didn't glow. And now they've got babies with techni-coloured noses. But they don't glow. And they don't fly us for the present delivery any more and their kids can hardly believe the stories old Rudolf tells, like, their dad's a big, old gasbag. Which he is, but that's a whole other story. And he has a bad case of gas going all the time too, by the way. But I digress from my woes.

Anyway now we're loading up the Flyarri. It's really cool, I'm dying to drive it, but of course I'm not allowed yet, I've got to wait till I'm like an old man of eighteen. What a waste. So we need to hurry, we're behind schedule already and we haven't even started. My old man comes scurrying down the icy path, with an armload of presents. Mom's scurrying after him, carrying even more stuff, but telling him not to carry so much, his back will go. And then, of course, dad slips, the presents fly straight into mom's path and she slips too. Whump! I hear the sounds of them go down. Thump for my dad, who is round, and Thwack for my skinny mom!

And now I've got to cut a long story short. As I said, we're, like, late already and now we're shorthanded, without our main act, since dad's back is out of whack and mom's not too good either. And they're really, really bad patients. Like, patient is a bad word to describe them when they're not well. They're not patient at all. Anyway, now they're trying to control operations from their respective beds. And now I've got to be main delivery boy. No, no, this isn't a dream-come-true story. I don't get to drive the Flyarri. We've got to get the reindeer and the old gig out and fly there the old way. Old Rudolph's little fawns are kicking and screaming that they want to go too. They can't, they're too little and he's too old to fly, he's probably forgotten how to, anyway. So we've got to go out on this really foggy night to do this without lights or anything. We hitch up some of the other flying reindeer, some of whom are muttering under their breaths about animal rights. I tell you, these guys . . . no one talks of child rights with us.

Anyway, back to cutting a long story short . . . now, we're like, set up and up, up and away! I can't see a thing, the fog is so thick, and it's like driving through cotton wool! And then there's a miracle, red lights glow and puncture the fog, clearing the way ahead. I look around, what could it possibly be? Has Rudolph come along? But no! Would you believe it—it's my little cousin's pimples—they're like glowing like fog lights. He looks pretty weird with bright red beams sparkling out of his face, but well, it's going to get us there. I guess pimples have their uses after all!

So, my advice is, stay up this Christmas night and keep a watch out of your window. You'll get a treat—a sleigh flown by reindeer, with fried egg pimples for headlights, all being flown by a green-stockinged Santa's not so little helper!

Hope you get what you wished for . . .

THE END

And would you believe it, I won! I won the competition! Good to know old PF Panda (as in pimple faced, remember?), has a sense of humour. In fact, she made me read it in front of the whole class. And they were tossing about, laughing. It was crazy. I got thumped on the back and that's not all I got. That prize that Panda had promised? Would you believe, it was an iPod, given by an organization that was promoting creativity! And a chance to participate in an international online essay competition. That was so cool.

When I got home, there was more good news. Dad said the doctor says he can travel in a week. We're going to go on that trip after all! I guess my dad's not so bad after all. In a way, I did get what I wished for, in a roundabout way.

Jason Jamison and I

'FORTY LOVE.'

Game to Jason Jamison!

Jamison! He looked like a Greek god. Flowing, almost blond hair and deep blue eyes. How had the principal allowed him to keep such long hair? He was one of those tanned, athletic types who make life difficult for all of us lesser mortals. He prowled the baseline now, as he waited for me to serve out the match. He had hardly worked up a sweat, which wasn't surprising considering I had made so many unforced errors and served enough double faults to hand him this crucial inter-house tennis match in our school tournament.

I turned back to my service line. Involuntarily my eyes strayed to my house bench. I was met with glum looks of disappointment and betrayal. As though I was purposely doing this. I hung my head down and tried to swallow the painful lump in my throat. I bounced the ball and glanced up. Tears prickled behind my eyes and blurred my vision. I shrugged my shoulders, trying to ease the knots of tension. As I braced myself for the toss-up, I felt my hand tremble.

Damn! I hoped it was just a small tremble that Jason Jamison hadn't noticed. I breathed deeply, gritted my teeth, tossed the ball up, let my free hand follow the line, and then swung the racquet, putting all my puny weight behind it.

'FAULT!'

'Sh . . .' I cursed under my breath. The lineswoman was a young lady teacher and I bet she, along with all the other females there, was swooning over my Greek god opponent. Giving him the benefit of close calls. I stared hard at the point where the ball had bounced near the line, the way I'd seen Roger Federer and others do. But it made no impression on anyone. I was asked to continue. I geared up for my second serve. Again the slight tremble.

'FAULT!'

Well, to cut a long and pathetic story (or nightmare) short, I handed the match in my service game, to Jason Jamison. A big roar from the crowd accompanied the final smash which fell on my court like a guillotine on my pride. He was coming over now. Fair hair flowing, Nadal-like and shaking my hand. But I was numb and felt as though I'd been put into iron bands. From somewhere far away, I could see myself shaking the referee's hand, packing my kitbag and walking away, trailing after a swaggering Jason Jamison. I didn't dare look up towards my house benches which were awfully quiet.

Two girls jumped a fence ahead of us as we neared the changing rooms.

'Hi Jase, congrats!'

'That's great, Jason!'

Adoring eyes shining up at him and fingers brushing his arm—as if by accident. And he, smiling back. White, even teeth, a pretender's bashful smile. I had to get away. I felt nausea rising up inside me. The path was narrow and those fawning girls blocked the way.

'. . . coming to the inter-house dance, Jase?'

My head was pounding, my vision swimming.

'E-excuse me . . .' I stammered from somewhere far away, fighting to keep the nausea down.

'Huh? Oh Gaurav? Never mind yaar, better luck next time . . .' purred one of the silly females, pushing up next to Jamison, pretending it was just to let me pass.

And pass I did. Pass right out. Right there on the ground. At the very feet of the Greek god and his adoring worshippers. I slipped into blank blackness. Oh the shame of it! The last nail which sealed the coffin of my self-respect—my confidence. I couldn't face the world, couldn't even face myself.

Luckily (and quite understandably) I'd been replaced in the doubles match. I felt ill with self-reproach and guilt. That night on that hard hostel bed, my sleepless dreams were filled with replays of the match. Every serve, every shot, every fault ran and re-ran in my head. If only I did this. I could have done that. I should have . . .

My schoolmates would hardly speak to me next morning, avoiding my gaze every time I saw them in the corridors. Even Arjun, my cousin and friend, who slapped me on my back saying, 'It's okay, yaar, it's only a game,' lacked conviction in his voice. I wished I could have gone home, but I was a hosteller. I was stuck.

My world was darker than it had ever been before. I had been the main hope of my house. I'd been in top form. I'd hardly ever lost a match. And I was slated to become the school tennis captain—keeping up the tradition of my father and mother and uncle who'd all captained some sports team in this school. All was on course, until this cursed Jason Jamison came to join school. God, he really had it all, didn't he? Looks, style, height and a devastating serve.

I sighed and dragged myself into the bath, locking the door after me. I looked at the sorry face that stared back at me from the mirror. Big eyes, bigger ears, sunken cheeks. No, it wasn't an athlete's face, more like those faces they show on television from famine-struck third world countries. I'd never make it into the Greek god category.

At last they came, hot tears like molten lava that seared down my face. My sorrow engulfed me and my body was wracked with sobs. It isn't often a boy my age gives himself up to tears. I am, after all, fifteen and almost a man.

Afterwards, I felt even more miserable and ashamed. Crying is supposed to help. But it didn't help me any.

Quietly I slipped out of the bath, hoping not to bump into

anyone. Like a shadow, I crept past the hostel buildings and warden's office. I slipped behind the common room. Here a clump of bushes gave one a fairly good protective covering, almost hidden from view. I came here sometimes. It was my secret haven and I had told no one about it, not even Arjun.

I leaned against the cool, moss-covered wall and drew my knees up against my chest, resting my chin on them. My mind was a confused whirl of thoughts. I didn't know how I was ever going to come to terms with my humiliation. Too late, I heard the footsteps. Glancing up, I saw the dreaded Jason Jamison. Quickly I tucked my head between my knees, hoping he'd go away, leaving me for asleep, or even dead! I hated playing ostrich by hiding, but I wasn't up to anything else.

'Just go away . . .' I urged mentally, silently. Hating him with every fibre of my being.

'Hi!' a deep, throaty voice that sounded as though it should have a guitar accompanying it. *Mine hadn't finished breaking yet and would squeak every now and then.*

Reluctantly I looked up to find him flopping down next to me. I cursed him silently. Obviously one of the few things he didn't have was good manners. He could plainly see that he was intruding.

'Man, what a cool place you've found.'

Now he'd spoilt that for me too. I knew I'd never find my peace here again. Now that he'd been here. I didn't answer him, just tucked my head back into my knees. Damning myself for playing ostrich. I actually had never wanted to hit anyone as badly. But I knew he could pulverize me, the way he had on the court. He was already a man and I was half-man, half-boy—and not much of either.

He was quiet for a while, then put his hand into his pocket and pulled out a packet of gum. 'Want some?'

I shook my head, keeping my mouth shut, knowing if I said anything now, given my luck, my voice would shake or squeak. He put the pack away, not taking one for himself either. He stretched out and sat there. Quiet. I studied him through the corner of my eye. Laid-back, cool. Content. He seemed to be everything that I was not, but strove to be. And that made my dislike for him more acute.

'I-uh-I was looking for you, actually . . .' he started.

'*To gloat, I bet,*' I thought.

'I'm sorry about the game, man, I really am.'

I looked up at him sharply. But he was looking away into the distance.

'S-sorry? Why should you be sorry?' What was he up to?

'Well, it can't have been easy for you to lose out to a newcomer like that. I'm really sorry.'

'Hey, you're the better player. You're the big star now. You don't have to worry your pretty head over me!' I couldn't help my stupid little outburst. I was embarrassed of myself even as I said the words. But I wasn't about to apologize.

'I believe you're used to winning. I believe you've never lost much,' he continued, still addressing the distant spot he seemed riveted by. 'But you know, losing is something worth getting used to.'

I should have hit him right there and then, not worrying about the consequences. But he suddenly turned to face me. Putting his hands up, he quickly said,

'I'm sorry. I'm really, really sorry dude! I didn't mean to come over so preachy. The last thing you want now is a silly lecture. Are we cool?' He put his hand out and repeated the apology. I couldn't figure him out at all. But something sad danced in his eyes, so I took his hand and shook it and mumbled something. I'm not sure what.

'Thanks,' he said, 'I'm not sure I'd have been able to forgive that little lecture I laid on you, if I'd been in your place.' He laughed, shook his head and said, 'I swear, I don't know what comes over me sometimes.' Then he lapsed into silence again. I waited for him to say something. The silence was beginning to get embarrassing. But he was quiet. So I ventured, 'You were looking for me?'

I couldn't figure him out at all. What was it he wanted? I got a strange feeling that he wanted to say something more than merely sorry. But he was also avoiding it, whatever it was. 'Yeah, um . . . look . . . that Doon team is coming for the sports meet. I haven't asked coach yet, but I thought I'd ask you first. Could both of us team up for the doubles?'

'What?'

He started explaining, asking me if I would be his doubles partner at the Meet.

'But, but Jamison, what are you talking about?'

He began to patiently explain a third time, but I interrupted him, 'Look, I know what you're saying, but . . .'

'But what?'

'But why are you asking me?'

'You're slated to be the next captain, aren't you?'

'No! No! That was in the past. I *was* slated to be captain. But after today, it's sure to be you.'

'Hey man, I wouldn't dream of taking your place. I'm just a newcomer here.'

'Jason, it isn't yours for taking and it isn't mine for the giving. The coach will decide and he's sure to pick you over me after the whitewashing you gave me today.'

'I don't know, not after just one match,' his voice was just a whisper, sad, almost, 'not after . . .'

'Not after . . . what?' I asked, trying to egg him on.

'Hmmm . . .?' he started, as if I'd interrupted him.

'Not after what, Jason?'

He laughed out loud. A harsh, forced, false laugh.

'Leave it, it's nothing. Well, I'd better go!'

He got up, abruptly, hurriedly, as if trying to cover his tracks, close the door he'd been about to open.

'How about some of that gum you offered earlier?'

I could hardly believe that I was suddenly trying to keep him from going.

'What? Oh yeah, sure,' Jason smiled, but I could see the mask slipping over, closing down on whatever he wanted to say earlier.

'You want to talk?' I asked, curious.

It took him a little while to open up again. You could see he was treading down a path of thorny memories. The pain and sadness was evident. But, slowly he began, talking in a bare whisper.

'I'm a very good tennis player, I know that. I also know that I probably deserve to be captain too, tennis wise. But—they know about me, so they're scared. Haven't you noticed that they've let me keep my long hair? The rest of you've got to keep yours regulation length?'

'So, you're saying they're scared of you?' that was pretty impressive.

'Well, not scared of me, I guess, but scared of the awesome job they have of putting right all the things that are wrong with me. All the things that are wrong in my "pretty head" as you put it! So I get a long hair concession.' He smiled ruefully.

'All the things wrong with you? What're you saying? The reason why I was so bummed out was because you . . . because you're too damned—well, perfect. Didn't you see how those girls were fawning over you after the match?'

'Yeah—girls. Yeah!' he smiled. 'A lot of times girls go for the way I look, phirang-like. My mother's Scottish, which explains my colour. But the way girls treat you, like you're special. Pretty soon you start believing you really are—above everyone else. My dad's family wasn't too keen on him marrying my mom, so he stopped meeting those from his past.

My mom, well she's a good tennis player. Not great, but very, very good. It was her life. She lived, breathed and ate tennis. In me she saw, not a son, but a future Wimbledon champ. I was her dream come true. Or something weird like that. Sort of living out her dreams through me. Something deep. That's not what I say, but one of the many shrinks I've been to. Anyway, this tennis legend in the making was never supposed to lose a match. She was mad about me becoming a tennis legend. She'd never let me lose a match. She'd actually beat me if I did. Once, she broke a racquet on my back—one of those old-fashioned wooden ones. She drove herself and me to tennis the whole time. Tennis, tennis, tennis. It was all we talked about. She would've entered my dreams just to make sure there was nothing in there but tennis.' Jason smiled ruefully.

I tried to imagine what that was like. But I couldn't. In my house, it was often the other way around. Although I came from a pretty sporty family, my elders would often say that I should not sacrifice my studies for the game. That preparing for exams was my first priority. But Jason was still lost in his painful memories, so I didn't interrupt.

'My dad was not as into tennis. In fact, I still wonder what it was that got them together in the first place. They had nothing in common. Anyway, the game drove a wedge between my mom and dad as well as between dad and me. Mom was a misfit because of tennis, because of being a foreigner. Dad was a misfit too—in his own community, because mom didn't like anyone of her in-laws. And of course, dad was a misfit, an outsider, in his own home. They fought a lot. Mostly over me—dad saying I should be spending time with studies, mom saying that I was so gifted and should not be burdened with mundane things like Math and Science. So finally, one fine day, she left us and went back to Scotland. Sometimes she desperately wants me back. There'll be this bunch of phone calls and late night text messages begging me to come to her, that she'll send me a ticket, that she'll get a bigger house. Whatever. The ticket never comes, though. Other times, she won't call for months. Nothing, not so much as an sms. Forgetting my birthday, sometimes. So my dad and I were left strangers to everyone around us and strangers to each other.

'Didn't you ever see your mom again?' I asked. This was a terrible story. I felt pretty guilty for all the crappy things I'd been thinking about this guy. I certainly didn't envy him any more.

'I saw her, occasionally. But dad couldn't afford to fly me back and forth so often and she couldn't either. So it's not often. Anyway, things really began to slide after she was gone. I had nothing but tennis which I hated because it had torn my family apart. I was lousy at my studies and good at nothing but this thing I hated so much. I went pretty berserk then. Smoking, drinking. Even drugs, a bit, well, quite a bit. I'd do anything and everything I could lay my hands on—eraser fluid, glue, even pretending to cough so I would be given cough syrup, which I'd gulp down in very large doses. The only reason the school didn't throw me out immediately was because I was still bringing in tennis trophies regularly. Then one day, the girl I was going out with left me. Said she was sick of my behaviour, the drugs and stuff. She said her parents disapproved of our relationship and would pull her out of school if she didn't break up with me.'

His voice was hoarse with pain and loss. The tears had escaped from the corners of his eyes and wet his cheeks. But he didn't seem to mind. Or perhaps he hadn't noticed. He was so lost in his nightmare.

'It broke me up, that. I couldn't take another loss. Well, I had a match that same afternoon with a real creep who I could beat with my eyes blindfolded and one arm tied behind my back. But I arrived drunk for the game. Of course, I was whitewashed in the first set. Then I threw up in the middle of the court as the second set started. Of course I was made to concede the match and dragged off. Disgraced. I couldn't stand the game and all that it had done to me.

'Anyway, a while later, I caught the guy alone—the one who'd won the match earlier. I beat him up real bad. I guess I was just taking out all the anger that had been pent up inside me. I beat him horribly. I broke his nose, took out a couple of teeth. I think. And then, naturally, I was expelled. Thrown out like an unwanted dog. A pariah. Ah! God . . .'

He curled himself up into a tight knot of pain. His fingers

stroked his head—he was used to consoling himself. I didn't know what to say, what to add.

'So you came to this school?'

He struggled to regain his composure as he went on. 'Yeah, my dad had to pull every string he could. The coach here had known my mom and had seen me play one of my real good matches, so he persuaded the principal to give me a chance. I'm on medication to keep me off all that stuff,' he shuddered. 'I hope I never go back to that again. It's a real rough ride! Besides, I'm on my last chance here. I know that if I blow things here, I'm a lost cause.'

I swallowed, finding a lump in my own throat. I couldn't help the admiration I felt at this moment. How much he'd been through, how much he'd had to overcome. And it was obvious that he was going to give an honest effort to come out of the mess he'd found himself in. He sat quietly now. Finally, I spoke,

'Look, Jason, maybe we should start practising for the doubles match. We haven't all that much time, have we?'

This time, when I put my hand out to shake his, there was no tremble. He nodded, 'Let's go, man.'

Hearing My Own Story

THERE HAD BEEN a horrible report in the paper that morning. Not that I read the paper in the morning. But some of my classmates had heard it on the news the previous night—'oh it was so awful . . . why do they show such gross things on TV?' and then there was a detailed story in the morning papers.

'I swear, can't we have good news, sometimes?'

Some of my classmates seemed almost close to tears. On the other hand, old Oddball Piya looked close to gleeful. There's something about bad news that gets her all excited. The worse the news, the better for Oddball. We all call her that, though none of us has the guts to tell her to her face, of course. We'd be the bad news that she'd gloat over next if she ever found out!

As I said, I hadn't read the news. And I hadn't watched it on TV either. My father watches in his study and I watch movies or serials on my computer. And of course, I don't see why I should be watching bad news or reading about it.

My life is all about Bad News and I don't need to supplement it with the world's woes. So, I had no idea what the others were talking about. Anyway, since it was all everyone was talking about, I soon got to know. It was yet another case of wife beating and torture. Like so many other stories. What made this one more news worthy and grabbed the attention of my friends was that it was more gruesome than the usual. I didn't even want to know the details. Violence sickens me. No, actually sickens me. I get physically sick —like pukey-sick.

I put it out of my mind. Or at least, I tried to. Not so easy, but school lessons will push real life out of your head like nothing else will, except maybe a test, which we had. A Sanskrit test, so I certainly wasn't concentrating on some poor, hapless tortured stranger. And then there was the Christmas vacation coming. And rumours of the break-up of a huge Bollywood couple that made us put the story of wife beating out of our heads. Well, out of my head, at least.

It wasn't until later that the topic came up again. It was in the last period. The class teacher's period. As vacation was nearing, there was no catch up work or anything so we decided to have a discussion. At first, when Sonya Singhania volunteered the topic of the wife beating from the news, a whole lot of us protested—including me. I mean, why not discuss something fun? But Mrs Lall, our teacher, seemed to jump at the first opportunity and then there was no budging her. But then she said, 'If you don't mind, I'd like to tell you a story first, and then we'll move on to the discussion, how's that?'

That cheered me up a bit. Mrs Lall's an awesome storyteller.

She started telling us this story about a boy and how he is witness to his bhabi being beaten every day. He feels angry but also helpless. How can he stand up to his elder brother? But the way he turns away from the violence, kind of blind-siding it. Made my blood run cold.

I felt my hands go numb. I felt myself begin to shake. Just like the boy in the story. I was him. I could feel the nausea rising up my throat. I could feel the classroom darken and recede. I gritted my teeth as the boy in the story disappeared too. And was replaced by me. I found myself there, smack in the middle of the story. And it wasn't someone's bhabi whose skin was blue from old bruises and red from brand new ones. And it wasn't an elder brother who was hitting. Hitting. Hitting. Oh God! No! No!

I opened my eyes in panic. I tried to stop the images. I tried to keep down the nausea. No one must know. No one must know. This was my dirty little secret and I could not let it out. It was my duty to keep it secret. *Family matters must not be discussed openly on the outside. Secrets* . . .

But the images would not stop. It was as if Mrs Lall was telling *my* story. My story to the whole class. Stop! I wanted to shout out. It's a secret. My secret. It's not your story to tell. But she wouldn't stop and the images would not stop.

He's coming back for her again. His hand is raised, his eyes bulge out of his head in rage and his face is flushed. Sweating. He has the same glee shining in his face. It's radiant, as though he's really, really enjoying this. And I? Well I'm curled up in my corner, as usual. My eyes are closed. My hands are over my ears. See no evil. Hear no evil. Do no evil. Evil, evil, evil . . . I chant to myself. Cutting out the cutting, slapping, hitting sounds. And then the moaning, crying, weeping sounds. I shield myself from it all. I won't hear this evil and I won't see this evil. And there's nothing I can really do to prevent this evil. I'm a child. Just a child. And they're not only grown-ups, but my parents too. I have to obey them. They are supposed to protect me. I am not supposed to protect them. That is not my brief. So I shut them out. Cut them out and pretend that what's happening isn't happening. At least not to me.

I know that the rest of the day and the days after will follow the same set pattern of a hundred times before.

Either one or other of my parents will be seated at the table, at lunch or dinner or whichever cursed meal it happens to be. Then they'll be broody, the anger, the hurt simmering still. We'll eat quietly. I'll be told to eat, put your head down and eat what's put in front of you. So I do, because I've learnt that simmering anger can boil up again and this time it can be directed at me. My father, whose rage may not be completely spent. Or my mother, who does not, dare not say a thing to her violent husband will take out her pent-up rage and anguish on me. I understand it, I guess. But I assure you it does not make it any easier for me to bear.

I feel the tears of helpless rage prickle in my eyes. My

throat is tight with a lump of anger, or grief, or whatever. I feel so alone, so alone. There's no one who I can share this dirty secret with. Family secrets must remain within the family. But when the secret is to do with the family itself, then . . .?

I see Raima put her head down on the desk, I see her hands tremble as she covers her ears, trying to block out the discussion. As a teacher, I'm supposed to discuss a topic from the newspaper. I thought this one would be a good topic to discuss with a class full of young girls on the verge of becoming women. But seeing one of my students crumbling before my very eyes, I'm not sure any more. Is it any of my business to talk about this? I should just have stuck to my syllabus. I wish I had. That's safe—learning about kings and queens of long ago is less painful than the wars that children have to face today.

I am forced out of my thoughts, by Deepali asking in her big, aggressive voice, 'What's wrong with the wife, why doesn't she just leave the bastard?'

Everyone gasped. She'd used such a word. One that we all knew, of course, and many used, but not in a classroom, in front of a teacher. But Mrs Lall just smiled. She's like that. 'Yes,' she said, ignoring the smirky looks from everyone else. 'Yes, Deepali, I understand your anger, your amazement, even. It is indeed strange that she would just stay in such a violent marriage.'

'Cool it yaar,' that was Oddball with a disgusted look at Deepali who she was convinced was a wimp, 'Cool it, dude, it's just a story, stop getting so worked up about it.'

'It is *not* just a story, Piya, that's just the point. Isn't that the point of your telling us this story, Ma'm?'

That, of course, sparked off a huge debate in class. And Mrs Lall just had to concentrate on keeping some semblance of order and quiet so that it wouldn't disturb the other classes.

I was glad that the crowd grew unruly and I could head off the discussion with trying to get them back to order. There were often teachers who complained that the noise from my classroom disturbed their classes, so I had to be extra careful.

Raima was rocking herself slightly backwards and forwards. Luckily there was enough chaos in the class to keep the attention off her. I hoped no one would loudly call my attention to her.

I lost the thread of the discussion, because now my mind was full of confusion. And yes, full of fear too. It may sound stupid, but it had never occurred to me that my mother should leave. That she could, in fact leave. Suddenly the spectre of divorce reared its ugly head. Despite the fact that things had been really, really bad in my house, somehow I'd never thought that she could one day decide to leave my father. Would she leave me too?

I saw Raima shake herself. As though she was shaking off some horrible thoughts. She glanced up and met my eye, and then she looked back down into her lap immediately. No, this was not something that could be brought up in front of the whole class. But I knew, now that I had inadvertently scratched at a deep wound, I would have to try and heal it too.

I shook myself, 'stop it.' I concentrated on Mrs Lall, on

her words. I forced myself back into the present, into the classroom. Telling myself, this is just a story, just a story.

Mrs Lall was saying, 'Now, this is just a story, but Piya, your question is valid. But why do you think that the woman who has been written about in the news didn't just leave her husband if he was so violent?'

'She was too dumb,' sneered Piya, egged on by the teacher's validation of her point. 'If I'd been in that wimpy wife's place, I'd just have killed the idiot and got on with my life.'

A whole lot of my classmates cheered, most were laughing. I felt a twinge of regret and a whole lot of relief. The discussion would now deteriorate into foolishness. And I'd be safe.

But our teacher was not going to let this one go the way of foolishness.

'I've no doubt that you would do some such thing. And of course, there have been cases of the wife killing her abusive husband.

'Ya, ya, remember? There was a movie about it even. Aishwarya Rai acted in it.'

'She looked so bad without her make-up and all, no?'

'Shut up Naina, don't be such a dumb blond. The woman's being bashed up. She's just killed her husband. The last thing she'd be worried about is putting on make-up. Mad yaar.'

'But Ma'm in that movie, after she's killed her horrible husband, she gets sent to jail. How dumb is that?'

So I explained to them, as best I could with my limited knowledge about the law. And that killing is still killing and while a strong case can be made, often there is lack of evidence. And such. But I knew that my job was not over yet. So I went on . . .

'But as you know, domestic violence is not a rare thing. It's terribly common. Some statistics show that one in every five women has faced some violence. So why is it that these women don't kill their husbands, as Piya so forcefully puts it—or at least, leave them? Why do you think that's so?'

My blood froze over. Why did my mother not leave my dad? Was it because of me? Is it because she couldn't make a life for herself without him? Is it that she couldn't afford my school fees and stuff and that's why she kept putting up with the horror of her life? And did my dad know this—and that's why he kept perpetrating this crime against her? Was it, after all, my fault? My fault?

I couldn't stop the tears. I could feel them spilling out and as I sat there, my head down on my desk. I barely heard the next bit of conversation; someone said:

'Ma'm, on TV there are these ads for something called "Bell bajao andolan" or something.'

'Yah, yah, if you think that there's violence going on in someone's home, just go up and ring their front door bell.'

'How would that help?'

'Yeah! If the guy is that mad, he would start thrashing you instead!'

'No, no, the idea is to distract the guy from the moment. And also to let him know that there are other people around. People aware of what's going on.'

'Ma'm, if your stats are right and one in every five women are getting beaten at home, then five or six of us right here in the class have it happening in our homes too. But that can't be right, surely?'

'No, dummy,' someone else argued, 'it doesn't happen in our kind of homes, stupid, its like, amongst our maids and drivers and stuff, not our homes. Not *our* kind of homes.'

'Is it? Is that really, really so?' Mrs Lall spoke in her quiet, listen-to-me voice. The voice she used when she needed her class to listen very quietly and carefully. Her voice throbbed in my ears as the class fell silent.

'Isn't it?' someone asked. I could no longer tell who was talking. I just knew that my secret was coming closer and closer to the surface. I would be exposed. Would my parents be angry with me for letting the secret out? Would my father beat me for telling? Even if it was the truth?

The words of my classmates buzzed around me like bees. Intent on attack. I was trembling. And I think I was crying. But I kept my head down. Maybe no one noticed.

Then I heard Mrs Lall ask us, 'What else could the wife or children in a household such as this do?'

I listened. Yes, what could I do? Was there really something that I could?

The ideas tumbled around me and through the blur of tears I felt that maybe, yes maybe I didn't have to be a mute bystander. Maybe.

You get these spy cameras. You could put them around the

house and record the violence being inflicted so that you have proof.

Or even just a recording on your cell phone.

There are Crimes against Women cells. You could approach those.

And I've seen these ads for Mediation centres run by the government or police or something.

But for cameras and stuff you need money. Maybe the wife is not financially independent and so stays stuck there.

Yes, yes, I could see how my mother would feel that she had no option. She had never been able to have a job. My father never allowed it. But then I heard Mrs Lall say:

'The wife does not have to be financially independent. In a situation like this, the court will order the husband to pay maintenance. He is obligated to.'

I started to feel a little stronger, a little more positive. But I couldn't lift my head up as yet. I knew my face was stained with tears. But there were no tears now.

And then it was over. The bell rang. But I couldn't bring myself to look up as yet. I could not gather myself. I hoped no one would notice that I had my head down on my desk. I hoped everyone would just quietly leave. And leave me alone.

The class filed out of the room. Supriya, Raima's friend, suddenly noticed her sitting head down. She was about to go up to her. Supriya pointed at her, looking at me. I shook my head, put my fingers to my lips and indicated she should just leave quietly. I was not sure what I was going to do. It was obvious that domestic violence was a truth in Raima's home. Now that I had a strong suspicious about this, what was I, an outsider, her teacher, supposed to do?

I waited and waited. It became quiet. They'd left. I screwed up all the courage I had and lifted my head off the wood that was damp with my tears—stained dark like blood.

Mrs Lall sat at her desk, she seemed to be correcting some notebooks. But she looked up as I sat up. I had no words left. I felt drained.

'Are you all right, my dear?'

We're both tremulous, uncertain, but I go up to her and put my hand on her shoulder. She's looking older and more weary than any little child should look. I stroke her hair.

Mrs Lall strokes my hair, it feels nice, it eases the pain and tension. And then I can't stop it any longer. I throw my arms around her.

She throws her arms around me and sobs into my neck, her body shaking from the force of all her pent-up grief. She cries and cries and cries and I think I'm crying too. And then I can't stop the images that bubble up inside my head. The images kept buried for so many, many years. The raised hand, the bent back. My father beating my mother. My beautiful, gentle mother. He used to beat her when he was drunk. And I never did anything. I felt I never could.

I notice Mrs Lall holding on to me. I think that she is crying too. Why is she crying? I don't understand.

I wish I'd never read that story. Never thought to bring it up in class. I wasn't prepared for it to conjure up my own past. Never meant for it to cause pain to this little girl in my arms.

And finally, when we run out of tears, Mrs Lall lifts my face up. Her own cheeks are wet with her tears, but she wipes mine first. And she tells me about her own childhood. She tells me about the beatings of her own father. He used to beat her too. My father has never hit me, only my mother. But constantly, my mother.

We decide that we have to do something about this. Now that it is out in the open, Raima takes courage into her hands. She stands up firm, strong and states that she's going to take action. She's holding my face in her hands now.

'We will go to the police, Ma'm. I want to stop it. If you will come with me,' she says.

And I know, at last, that my ghosts can be put to rest too.

'I will go with you,' I say.

Like Smoke

SHE HUMS HER early morning song as she deftly packs the lunch for her mother and father. She's already pretended to have cooked her own, wrapping a plastic bag around a cloth duster so that it looks like a packet of food. She knows her mother is dead against her plan to diet, but Zeenat knows that she is getting fat. She's started hating looking at herself in the mirror. She felt her chin was wobbly and her cheeks too round. She sucked her cheeks in to give her that beautiful gaunt look that she loved. Her friend Farida had it. But then she also had that haunted look that came from too much loss. Yes, Farida was used to loss. She'd seen her own father and brother being dragged away in the late evening, never to return.

That way, Zeenat was lucky. Most of her other classmates had had similar violent losses in their families. Zeenat's family had been spared 'by god's grace', she muttered under her breath as she spooned rice and potato curry into her parents' tiffin boxes. She missed school. It had been months now that school had been shut by strikes, bandhs and curfews. She missed not going out now. Her parents went out every day, leaving her behind with warnings to lock the door, draw the curtains and pretend no one was home.

She was proud of the fact that her mother went to work too. She was a nursing assistant in a hospital nearby. It was hard work and often not a very rewarding one either. She was supposed to be in the delivery ward, but there weren't many babies being delivered nowadays. What with all the stress and tension that women lived with, they weren't conceiving babies. Not to mention that many, many men had been lost in all the violence that rocked their beautiful Kashmir valley at regular intervals, often peace being a very short interlude, between terrifying incidents of violence. So Ammi had been transferred into the Emergency ward. She didn't like this work. There were always gunshot victims and blast survivors coming in. And this disturbed Ammi a lot. Zeenat could tell what her Ammi's day was like even before she came home. For Zeenat spent a lot of time in front of the television, listening and listening to the news. There was very rarely good news.

Not much at all after that cute Kashmiri boy had won Indian Idol. Zeenat smiled at the memory. Her Abbu had scolded her when her mobile phone bill came then. Much higher than normal because of all the text messages she'd sent to vote for the boy. He was Kashmiri and besides, he was cute. Of course, Zeenat, being Zeenat, had ignored the stupid fatwas that had been issued by the extremist organizations. Warning Kashmiris not to show support for a traitor who turned his back on his Kashmiriyat by participating in an Indian program. 'Kashmir is not a part of India,' they urged.

To which Zeenat had replied—out loud—to an empty room, 'Well, there isn't a Kashmiri Idol, is there—so what is the poor boy to do?'

'Singing is against Islam, especially singing of these vulgar film songs.'

'If Allah had not meant for him to sing, he wouldn't have poured so much talent into his throat.' Announced Zeenat firmly turning her back on dire warnings as she sms-ed her way to an inflated bill and her father's scoldings.

But she'd forced Abbu to watch the finale with her. Of course they'd kept the volume low just in case 'someone' was listening. But she knew that all her friends were watching too as was half of Kashmir which was rooting for their candidate, ignoring the nay-sayers.

And Zeenat had thrown her arms around her father when he cheered and clapped unabashedly as their Kashmiri lad was crowned Indian Idol. She was as happy that he'd won as she was that her darling Abbu had watched. And cheered, not even bothering to keep his voice down.

Zeenat adored her father. Of course, she loved Ammi too, but her mother had become so morose. Dour, almost, as lines of tension pulled at her mouth so it could hardly shape a smile any more. It seemed to Zeenat that Ammi disapproved of her every time she laughed. After trying to get through the growing walls of disapproval, Zeenat had more or less given up. She had the solid presence of her father, who would laugh along with her in her every moment of joy. And Zeenat had a joyous laugh. Head thrown back, her head scarf slipping off, her hair unwinding, wanting to join into the engulfing pleasure. It was a mighty, splendid, infectious laugh that invited others to join in. And they most often did. Whether they wanted to or not, others caught and rode on the waves of Zeenat's laughter. Even Ammi. Sometimes. Turning away so that no one would see that she still had a smile left in her.

'Teach that girl to behave more demurely,' Ammi often implored her husband. But Abbu would put a protective arm around his daughter's shoulders and declare, 'If any one tries to subdue my bachchi's laughter, I'll make sure they never smile again. She is a heaven sent angel who brings laughter to this godforsaken land of ours. As long as I'm around, Zeenat must only laugh her mighty laugh.'

So Zeenat watched television almost all day long, listening for the rare bit of good news or looking out for news that would tell her what her mother's mood would be that evening. It was like watching a weather report. And often it warned, '*storm ahead*!'

If there had been a blast or shoot-out in their part of restless Kashmir, then Ammi would have spent the day in blood and her demeanour and dreams would be blood-soaked too. Of course, they'd suggested to Ammi that she find some other line of work, but Ammi knew that it was very important that she be available for those who needed her. Abbu and Zeenat would tread softly that evening. For loud sounds upset her mother. Zeenat would finish the cooking early as the sound of the pressure cooker's whistle startled her. Zeenat lovingly massaged her Ammi's temples and aching feet and she was careful not to laugh. Though Abbu and she would exchange quiet smiles, reassuring each other that happiness was not too far away. Even on a night like this.

There was only thing that Zeenat didn't like about Abbu. And that was his smoking. He smoked altogether too much. Although he pretended that he did not. It was the only thing that they quarrelled over.

That and school. Zeenat wanted to go to school. Desperately. But school here had become so unpredictable. Always shut. Their exams had not taken place for a year now. There was talk that all students would simply repeat their class this year again. But Zeenat did not want to repeat class 8. She'd already gained from it all that she could. She wanted to go to the 9th grade. She wanted to move a step closer to finishing school, to becoming the computer engineer she dreamed of becoming. She begged her parents to let her study in a school in Delhi, or one of the boarding schools that some of her classmates had gone to. But they would not let her go. Fear had seeped deep into their minds and hearts. It had set their bones hard against sending their precious daughter away. Better safe and uneducated than running risks in the great unknown. So Zeenat tried to study at home, but she was bored and besides, she was not allowed out of the house alone. Ever. She felt stifled. Surely, surely, she was safe enough? And that's why she was putting on weight. What could she do—she got no exercise, played no games. She often wanted to run, feel the crisp wintery air against her face, feel the wind rush past her ears that are too full of televised voices of doom.

But instead, here she is, face flushed from the stove instead of sunlight, packing up her parents' lunch so that they can go out into the world while she stays home, television for company. She turns to find her Abbu lighting up yet another cigarette, his third already.

'Abbu!' she admonishes. 'Abbu, you promised, you promised me you're going to stop smoking. Put that cigarette out, Abbu.'

'Sorry, sorry,' he says.

'What "sorry" Abbu? You always say sorry and then you do the same thing. No, Abbu jaan, put out your cigarette now.'

'Oh ho, what do you have against my one pleasure beta?'

'Haw! How can you say your one pleasure? Isn't this home a pleasure for you? Isn't the food Ammi and I cook for you a pleasure? Aren't I?'

'Acha bhai, sorry, sorry,' her Abbu smiles, holding both

his ears, his cigarette clenched between his teeth, 'sorry, I was wrong, of course, I have so much joy and pleasure, you're right. Okay, then let me ask you, what do you have against my one vice?'

'Come on Abbu, you know what's wrong with smoking. You're behaving like you've never heard of cancer or all the horrible things that can happen. Don't pretend now Abbu. Just Stop Smoking. Put it out.'

'Acha baba, let me finish this, then I'll not smoke another.'

'No, no, put it out.'

'Last, last, I promise, this is my last cigarette.'

'Promise?'

'Promise, sweetheart, promise. Now let me enjoy my last cigarette in peace.'

Zeenat hugs her father and hands him his lunch. She pulls his nose gently and whispers, 'Now remember now, that's the last one!'

He hugs her and kisses her forehead and heads for the door.

Zeenat watches her father's phiran clad back as he slips on his shoes; he waves once more before hurrying out of the door, pulling it firmly shut behind him, keeping the cold out. Not letting the damp mist enter the warmth of his home.

Zeenat hears the door bang shut.

And then she hears another bang—a sickeningly familiar bang.

'Abbu . . .' she wrenches the door open. Her father is

collapsed on the steps of their house. His blood flows into the melting snow, turning it pink. He has been shot. A jeep speeds away.

'Abbu!' she screams. The cigarette has sizzled out on the cold, wet.

'Ammi!' she calls out in despair, turning back into the house. She stops in her tracks.

The smoke from her Abbu's cigarette, his last cigarette still hangs in the air. Something as tenuous, as temporary as smoke still exists. But the solid presence of her father has disappeared.

Like smoke. Like smoke . . .

City Boy

IT'S OFFICIAL, MY life is over.

Done finished. Khatam. That's it. Thanks. Goodbye.

I'm not being overly dramatic or anything, which is something I'm always accused of being. Drama queen and all that. And I am that some times. *Some times.*

But not this time. This time it's like—done. My life is totally tote-ally over. And I'm pretty sure you'll agree with me too.

You see, we're moving. My father has been transferred. And not even to some cool place like New York or even, I don't know Istanbul or something. NO, he's been transferred to Bhatinda. I mean, what's in Bhatinda? Sounds creepy and slow. Watery and tasteless. Like a tinda. You know? One of those crazily horrible veggies that are so bad they're supposed to be good for you. How could anything so squishy and pulpy possibly be good for you? I mean, come on. That's what Bhatinda sounds like—tinda. Come to think of it, it's even worse. It's like a combination of bharta and tinda—

two of my least favourite veggies. Baingan, even the name evokes a dark purple, squishy thing. And it's not as if it sounds better in English, Brinjal—it looks and smells like what most things look next morning, if you know what I mean.

Bharta + tinda = Bhatinda = worst nightmare.

When dad came home and announced this news to us, I was so stunned, I couldn't speak. But my mom, she had plenty to say. She objected like mad. And then they had this huge fight. I mean HUGE. You see, she's a copywriter in an advertising firm and has a real busy lifestyle. She buzzes about quickly wrapping up stuff around the house, like it's an aberration in the real course of her life. A speed bump put there, probably by dad and me, purposely to slow down her real life. And her life is not her house, and only partly her family. She really comes alive when she's working, or talking about her work.

So for her, moving to Bhatinda is like death. She actually said that. To dad's face. Clever words. I could empathize with her totally. That's exactly what I'd want to say if I had the words. Or the guts. Which she does and I don't. Like if she's mad, she spews words like a volcano. Me, on the other hand, go silent and still—statue-like. I'm boiling inside, but I freeze over on the outside. Both physically and verbally.

So, anyway, they were having this huge, huge fight. She said, 'Fine, you go. I'm not going.' And he yelled back, 'Fine!' and they both stormed off. Leaving 'statuefied' me still sitting still and silent. Although inside, I was applauding and thanking my mom. Good, if she wasn't going, then I wouldn't go either, right? I mean, kids always stay with their mom, right? Like Lukes, my friend, Lokesh, actually, but who'd use a stupid name like that? His parents broke up. The divorce is under way and he's going to stay with his mom and visit his dad on weekends. Each one gets him for half the vacations and stuff.

Then it hit me like a sledgehammer. Did mom's saying 'you go, I'm not' mean they were splitting up? Oh no, that's not what I wanted, especially not over stupid Bhatinda. My home, their marriage was going to be killed by Bhatinda? Ok, I really needed to figure this out and make sure they didn't end up getting a divorce or anything.

I went to mom. She was crying, sitting at her desk, her laptop open, but nothing on it.

'Mom . . .?'

But mmpffff is all I got out of her.

Some days later, my parents sat me down. At first my heart was sinking into my Nikes. These past few days I'd like, lived in dread that they would soon be telling me that they were splitting. They had these grim expressions on their faces. They were giving each other guilty looks. Each one was trying to get the other to start, to take the plunge.

I waited. But they didn't say a word.

'Are you getting a divorce?' came shooting out of my mouth involuntarily. 'What?!!' they shouted together.

So okay, relief, relief. A divorce wasn't on the cards. But something almost as bad—BAD.

My mom had been offered a crazy good job, a hike in salary and position. It was going to be in London. But . . . BUT she couldn't take me. She was going to stay in a women's hostel and besides, schools and stuff were way too expensive there. And it was just for a couple of years or so.

'A couple of yeeerrrrrs? But that's a lifetime!' I wailed.

'Big picture, son, big picture,' my dad said. It's one of his favourite things to say. He always thinks I'm losing perspective and blowing things way out of proportion. Drama queen, he muttered under his breath. But I heard him. Hate when he says that. I mean, I am a boy, so couldn't he at least say Drama king? Sounds soooo much better!

So, bottom line—I was going to Bhatinda but *without* mom. Worse than before. Just a shade better than a permanent split between them, I guess. But only a shade. This was terrible.

'If I have to go, then you have to go too.' I tried to guilt mom to change her mind. But she guilted me back saying that she'd had this wonderful opportunity and it wouldn't be fair to take it away from her. And okay, it wasn't fair. But was it fair what they were doing to me? Then I had another idea.

'Okay, tell you what, since we're not going to be together anyway, why don't I go to a boarding school?' Anything was better than rotting in Bhatinda.

'Look,' said dad, 'I don't want you going to a boarding. I can't afford it anyway.'

'Well, maybe mom with her fancy new assignment can pitch in with my fees.'

'Son, I'd really, really like you to be with me. I know it won't be the easiest. But remember, it's not the easiest for me either. I'd really appreciate your company. Think of this as an opportunity for us to get to know each other better.' I could see that dad was trying to guilt me too. Well played, dad. No way could I say that I didn't want to spend time with him, now could I?

'Besides, we believe it will do you some good.'

'Good? Good how?' That tindas and Bhatinda is good for you story again. I hate the 'it's good for you' line, don't you?

'Well, it will give you the opportunity to explore a bit of the real India. It will get you out of the rarefied atmosphere of your city life, of mixing with people who are exactly like you. Treat it as an adventure.' That was mom doing her silver lining bit. Her 'always look on the bright side policy'. It set my teeth on edge.

'How about *you* exploring the real India instead of fancy foreign lands?' I shot back, then smiled a triumphant smile. How was she going to get out of that one?

'Son, I grew up in Jhalarapattan in Rajasthan. I know the real India. I did my degree in social work setting up health centres and libraries in villages. And that's how I know that it's something that's worth experiencing. Your father and I both believe that it's a great opportunity that has come your way at just the right time in your life.'

OHHHHH 'your father and I' . . . So, they were a team now! I mostly preferred it when they were on opposite sides of an argument. It left me out of it. When they're a team in the 'your father and I both think' kind of way, it leaves nowhere for me to run and hide.

'But it's going to be terrible for me to go to some lousy school. Think of all I'd lose out education-wise.'

'We've already found out. There's a very good school close to the house we're going to be in. It's a branch of one of the biggest schools of this city. So it's not going to be bad at all. They even have a swimming pool and horse-riding. You like that, don't you?'

Well, swimming and horse-riding sounded good. But suppose the swimming pool was a village pond passing off as a pool? And the horses could very well turn out to be tonga horses or shaadi vala horses.

My parents looked at me a long time. They could see that I wasn't going to be convinced so easily.

Mum sighed one of her famous sighs. And my dad stroked his chin and said, 'Son. I know you're not so happy about this. Of course you wish you could be in some fancy place with your mother. Or just where you are now. But I really would like for you to be with me. Besides, you know, it's just for two, two and half years. Before you know it, you'll be back in your old school. We are going to request them to hold your seat here.'

Ah see, this is how they trick you. First it was two years.

Now he was sneaking it in with a casual two, two and a half years. Before I knew it, I'd be going to college in the fair village of Bhatinda.

I knew there was no point in arguing. It was always going to be their decision. And they'd decided what was going to be good for me. They had no idea what it was going to be like for me when I came back. It would be just horrible. I could see it now . . .

'Where'd you go, dude?'

'Er . . . Bhatinda?'

I could already hear the jeering laughter. The disbelieving cries of, 'Is that even a place?'

Yeah, it was a punishment even though I hadn't done anything to deserve the punishment.

~

Well, mom came with us to Bhatinda. To help 'the boys' settle in. Sheesh, even *I* was hardly a 'boy' any more and balding salt and pepper, beer-bellied dad was certainly as far from a boy as he could be. And there was nothing much for her to do, frankly. Our cupboards were locked and transported. And we just had to put them into the various rooms and open them. And bam, we were as settled as we were going to be in the scintillating town of Bhatinda.

And then it was time for her to leave. It was horrible. You

could see that she was bursting with excitement to be off. Naturally, who could blame her? She was free of husband, son and Bhatinda all in one move. Smooth.

After she left, she went to stay at Nani's for a week. Her bags were already packed and there. I was going to miss her. And also miss the lifestyle she was going to be leading. Missing what I'd never known.

The school was not too bad, although my classmates were the pits—real village types. Oiled hair. Pants worn practically around their throats. In fact, one of them, thinking he was being helpful, offered to loan me his belt as he thought my pants were falling off. I tried to explain to him that only geeks and yokels wore their pants where he did. But I stopped myself. He was a geek AND a yokel. There was going to be no convincing him.

And the teachers were okay, but with terrible accents. I mean, I could hardly understand what they were saying. And it was pretty freaky when one of them said that I must learn to speak clearly as he couldn't understand me. I mean, same to you, dude.

Back home, it was pretty lonely. Dad was busy settling into his new job so he would stay at his factory till late. There were no friends who I'd want to invite home and none of them had invited me yet. To tell the truth, I didn't have any friends. As yet. And none that was on the horizon either. Sigh and double sigh.

I stared moodily out of the window. It was a pretty garden,

very green and ferny. But I wasn't really a garden type. I had brown thumbs that would turn any green plant to a weed. At least that's the kind of thing that happened when my mom tried to make me plant stuff on our balcony. She'd thought it would help me become a better human being or something, but in fact, I turned everything to dust. Literally.

So the garden was kind of nice to look out on to, but it wasn't my thing. That's when I noticed this kid sitting cross-legged on the grass. He was all alone, but he seemed to be talking. Some kind of nut. Wonder who he was. He threw his head back and I could hear a soft whistling sound. Then, he smiled broadly, nodded his head and continued talking and whistling. Weird. What was he talking to—voices in his head?

That's when I noticed that the bushes just near him were shaking and shivering. Was the bush responding to his talk? No, I shook my head, no, that was just too weird. Even for Bhatinda. The kid stretched his arm out. Holding it steady in front of him. Then a very strange thing happened. A little brown bird. One of those ordinary dusty ones, hopped out of the bush and came towards him. It stopped just a foot away from his outstretched hand, cocking its head this way and that. Hmm. It hopped closer and closer. And then, the most awesome thing. It actually hopped right on to the kid's hand! He was talking away to the bird, his head bobbing bird-like as well. As though it were climbing a ladder, the bird hopped up and up his arm. Unafraid as though it was used to this stuff. It reached his shoulder and gently pecked at the kid's ear. He giggled, then pulled something out of his shirt pocket. It was some food, for the bird pecked at it right out of his hand. After a bit, the bird hopped to the other shoulder, then made its way to the pocket and stuck its head into the pocket, helping itself to the food that was hidden there. Cool! I had to meet this guy.

I raced down the steps and I charged right up to where he sat. Suddenly he turned on me angrily—a curse on his lips, fury in his eyes.

'Who the hell do you think you are?' he barked at me in Hindi.

I pulled up short. What? Who did he think I was? This was my house. My dad's house. And my dad was the big boss here. Who the hell did this villager think he was?

'What're you doing in my garden?' I yelled back.

'It's not your garden. It's mine. It's my pitaji's!' he snarled. 'Go on, get out, you're not wanted here. You . . . you've spoilt everything!'

'What? What? What?' what was this crazy animal talking about? *His* garden? His *father's*? And anyway, what had I spoilt? I hadn't done anything, touched anything. This guy was a lunatic.

'You're a lunatic!' I spat at him, twirling my finger next to my head to illustrate what I meant, in case he didn't understand my words, villager that he was.

'Go away, go away, go away!!!' he shouted again.

This was too much. I mean, even if it was Bhatinda, it was still my house, my garden. I stepped up to him, pushing him. It wasn't really hard a push, but he reeled back and fell with a thump to the ground.

And he let out a fiery gaali— a filthy one. One that I knew but had never dared to even mutter out aloud. Although, I had used it under my breath on occasion. But this twerp just hurled it at me, scrambled to his feet and fled. I stood there, too stunned to react. No one had ever cursed me like this before. With such a filthy word! I was seething. I swore that I was going to find out more about the guy. If he did live here, why, I'd get him thrown out. And if his pitaji thought he owned this place, I'd set that record straight. I mean, Bhatinda or no Bhatinda, this was MY plot of land.

But then, life caught up and I forgot about him. I had this stupid project to do. On birds. I mean. What an idiotic, rural type of project was this? I was in class 8! I mean, *birds*?! Like ok, they're these sometimes pretty things that fly. And they make an awful racket early in the morning especially on a weekend, when you're trying to sleep late. I mean, what's to know about birds? And for boys my age. Like, give us something *sensible*, like volcanoes and rockets or something. Really, the teachers here had no idea about kids my age. Or maybe that's how kids were here. Idiots forever.

I sighed. I knew I had to, had to do well. I mean, I hate to admit it, but I've never been a great student. I exist in the lower middle class—on marks and grades, I mean. But here, I thought, I'd better get my act together and do well. After all, I was the smarter one in every way. I'd better show it in my marks too. Those are the things that count. In any case, I was a lot smarter. My English was better and there was no way I was going to be beaten.

So okay, birds. Now what kind of project would be cool for birds? Hmmm! There wasn't a lot I knew. I'd google something. So I logged on. But the server was down. Ah! The joys of Bhatinda. Now what? We'd been given a week for the project. But I hadn't got around to it earlier. And now it had to be submitted tomorrow. What was I going to do? I knew dad would be useless. He doesn't know much about birds and nature and stuff. That's more mom's department. Should I try to call her? But I guess with the time diff and the cost of a call, there wasn't much chance. And of course I couldn't Skype her either, without the Net.

I was pretty much on my own. I stared moodily out of the window. Maybe a bird would fly into my sights and I could observe it. Yeah, not a bad idea. A case study of a single bird. Or something.

Then I saw the brat again. The cursing one. Coolly sitting cross-legged in front of the same bush as yesterday. On *my* lawn. He had some nerve, showing up again after he'd been so rude to the sahib's son. I was about to leap off my chair and go charging out to tell him to get off my property, when I saw him whistle softly and hold his hand out. Once again, a bird hopped out. And then another. And another. It was so cool. He just sat there and the birds hopped right up to him. On to him. On to his arm. On to his shoulder. And peeped into his pocket. He seemed to be talking softly too. And in between raiding his pocket, the birds seemed to be listening to his words. Their heads were cocking from one side to another. I could faintly hear them cheeping and peeping in answer. Could they really be talking to him? Awesome. But he had been so rude and yelled and cursed me out. I'd lose face now if I went back to him. So I just sat there. Dying to go and see this closer. But I had my dignity. So okay, I'd just look for now, from my room.

The bush was alive with birds. Then I noticed some other kinds starting to gather—with plumed heads and red bottoms. They made really lovely piping sounds. I realized I was holding my breath. I was almost bursting when an even more awesome thing happened. Four or five little birds hopped on to him. He was almost covered with birds now and they were all talking to him. I had to get to know him better.

After a bit, I heard a woman calling. The boy gently began to move. But the birds didn't take fright. They reluctantly flew off him, some even followed as he called out, 'Aaya ma,' and started to run towards the servants' quarters at the end of the garden.

I had to investigate this. It was nothing like anything I'd ever seen before. I went to the kitchen where Ram Dev was making dinner. He was sure to know. He'd been working here for dad's predecessor as well. But he was a grumpy old guy and I knew I'd have to butter him up a bit. You know, get on his good side. I knew I hadn't really been on his good side since we'd arrived. Trouble was, he was a dal, roti, subzi kind of cook. He couldn't make any of the food I really liked—you know, pasta and bakes and stuff. And it is not as though there was a takeaway that would deliver pizzas when you felt like it. Anyway, although he probably couldn't understand English, he most likely knew that I was grumbling about his food. He'd given me enough dirty looks. But now I needed him, so I slid up to him and began, 'Namaste Ram Dev bhaiya, what's for dinner, its smelling sooooo good.'

He gave me yet another of his famous grouchy looks, 'Bhindi,' he answered monosyllabically.

'Yummm, my favourite,' I persisted. It actually was one of the few veggies I liked, so it wasn't a total lie. 'Could you teach me how to make it, please?'

'What, now?' he turned to look at me in shock.

'No, no. Not right now, I can see you're busy, maybe some other time.' I said hurriedly least he started expecting me to start cooking. Now was as good a time as any, so I casually asked, 'Ram Dev bhaiya, who is that little boy who sits in the garden?'

'Why?' the old man gave me a suspicious look.

'I don't have any friends here yet, so I thought I could be friends with him. He doesn't seem to have friends either.'

'He has all the friends he wants. You won't like him. He's not your type.'

I felt like yelling at him right then and there, telling him he had no right to decide what type I was or who I should be friends with. I felt like telling him that there was no one of my type in this godforsaken village. He must have seen the look on my face for he softened. He put a hand on my shoulder and said, 'Dekho, beta, I only mean that that boy, Rohit, well he's had a hard time in life. He doesn't have parents, he had to drop out of school and he's being brought up by the gardener who works here, but I don't know how long he's going to be able to keep him. You see, the gardener's wife has her own children and does not want the additional responsibility. So sometime, sooner rather than later, that boy is going to have to go.'

'But where will he go?' I asked, horrified. How could this kid be in such a situation and still have the patience to talk to birds?

'He is an amazing child,' Ram Dev said, smiling.

'I know, I've seen him with the birds—I've never seen anything like it before.'

Ram Dev's bhindi almost burnt, he was so involved in chatting with me, so he shooed me out of the kitchen. I walked out into the garden, quietly this time.

But as I rounded the corner to where he sat, I saw he already had one hand up, wagging a finger at me. As if he'd known I was coming before I came. It stopped me in my tracks and he nodded a slow approval. He continued cheeping and chirruping with the birds. And yes, they were answering him, or saying something. He even seemed to understand.

Then he turned his head slowly, grinned at me and beckoned me with his finger, asking me to come and sit down with him. I approached cautiously, slowly. The birds stopped their tweeting. They hopped around so that they were facing me as I came towards them and the boy. But when I was a few feet away, one of them took fright and let out a cry of alarm and flew back to the safety of the bushes. And the others followed. I stopped. I was sure he'd be all mad again and start shouting and cursing. But he didn't. He scowled a bit, though and I didn't know what to do. I mean, I did not want to back down just because a mere village kid was wagging his finger at me as though he was training a dog. But yet, I knew that what I'd seen from the window was something awesome. Something I'd never seen before. I wanted to know more about this bird boy. I stood stock still until I noticed his finger drop and his hand wave out to me.

'Aao, aao,' he said, gesturing for me to come sit next to him. I went. I sat next to him, wanting to ask, but not quite knowing where to start. I didn't want him to start cursing me out again. And I didn't want it to seem that I was prying into his life. The birds watched from a distance. He grinned at me. We both sat quietly, sizing each other up. Finally, I couldn't take it any longer. I'm not good with long silences.

'How do you do it?' I asked.

'There's nothing to it,' he assured me, knowing of course what I was asking. 'You just have to be still and you have to give them a friendly feeling. You just have to find shanti, that's all.'

'Who is this Shanti?' I asked, I hadn't seen any girls here. I didn't know who he was talking about. But he laughed, giggled, into his hand.

'Shanti's not a person, silly. I mean—shanti—peace. You have to find an inner peace. It helps you in stillness.'

I looked at him. I mean what was he, some kind of guru or sage? I'd never heard anyone so young talk about inner peace, for goodness sake. But as I looked at him, I was struck by the fact that there really was a peaceful quality about him. He really did have inner peace. I don't think I'd ever seen anyone with that quality before. A stillness that was not just absence of movement but a quality that came from inside the person. As though he was not bothered about the turmoil his life was in. I knew that I certainly did not have anything like it.

'But will they come to me?' I asked doubtfully.

'Why not?'

I didn't know how to answer that. But it set me thinking. Why would they not come to me? Could inner peace be taught? Could I learn it?

'Can you teach me how?'

'How to get inner peace, you mean?'

I nodded.

'Hmmm! I don't think I've ever tried to teach anyone before. But, okay, let's try.' He grinned. He looked like an ordinary boy then, just like me, in many ways, I realized, although I'd never have thought that a little while ago.

'I think you just have to be happy.' He made it sound so simple. I thought about it. Well, I was happy, in one kind of way.

'Aren't you ever sad or unhappy?' I asked. 'Aren't you ever angry? Aren't you worried about, about er . . . everything . . . And if you are, do the birds not come then?'

'Yes, of course I'm not always happy. But what I'm talking about is not just jumping around, laughing like a maniac kind of happy. I'm talking about being happy right now, right here. At this moment, for now. Being satisfied with the place I'm in.'

'So, you're happy just living in Bhatinda, not going to school, not even, not even having a family of your own?' there, I'd said it. I hoped he didn't mind. That I knew. That I'd said it out loud.

'Yes,' he said simply, 'I am happy. But that doesn't mean that I don't want more out of life. I want to go to school. I used to go to school you know. I used to study hard when I went and I was good at my studies. But now, I try and learn the best I can. So that I can get different kinds of jobs. I'd like to go to the city and work in an office. Those are things I'm working towards. But just because I don't have them yet doesn't make me unhappy. In fact, my happiness gives me strength, makes my path clearer. My anger and unhappiness weaken me, they cloud my path ahead and make me lose my way . . .'

'You sound like a god-man, a guru or something,' I said, a bit awed by all this wisdom coming from such a little, homeless, parentless village kid. He laughed out loud, 'I'm no god-man, bhai, I just love birds, that is all. Now, let's be still and try and be peaceful and see if the birds can be persuaded to come back.'

As we sat there, the boy and I, I thought of all the things that had been making me unhappy. Being in Bhatinda, my mother going away, my life changing. And then I saw that it wasn't such a bad deal at all. After all, my parents were doing well. Each one was realizing their ambitions, their dreams. And, although I'd never admit this out aloud, maybe this *was* 'good for me'. Maybe I was seeing things and meeting people I'd never have met in my old life. I felt the redness of my resentment leave me slowly. My body relaxed to the extent that I wasn't aware of it any longer. As I slid into it, I know a thought popped into my mind: 'Achieving inner peace should not be this easy'. But I was too far gone to attend to the thought.

Besides, a tiny rustle in the bush in front of us drew my attention. I almost tensed, but saw my friend look at me from the corner of his eye. I relaxed, still. And the little bird hopped clear of the foliage, came tweeting up, eyeing me and asking the boy if I was safe. He smiled, and I smiled too. That's when I felt the tug. Without moving I glanced at what was tugging at the pocket of my shorts. There was a little brown bird pecking away, perhaps looking for the chocolate that was always there.

I felt myself bursting with joy. What a story I'd have to tell my friends back in the city. But then I felt a twinge of regret. Going back to the city would mean leaving here, leaving my new friend, the birds. I was a new person now. And I wasn't in a hurry to get back to the city.

I talked to my father about Rohit. We got him enrolled into my school. My father made a bank account for him so that he'd have his own money and not have to depend on someone else. Once the money pressure was off, the gardener and his wife were more than happy to have him stay on as part of their family.

I think it is going to be okay—as long as we have the birds.

And, by the way, I did really well on my bird project. I took pictures of Rohit covered with birds and about all the birds and their bird boy had taught me. I Skyped ma and showed her the project. And she was clever enough not to say, 'I told you so'.

Those Yellow Flowers of August

I HATE MUSLIMS. I always have. Well, almost always. Ever since I learnt what Muslims were. These people who are as black as the clothes they wear. Long black beards for the men. Black shrouds for the women—shrouds, as if they are the walking dead. Just those suspicious eyes peering out at the world give any indication that they're not dead—which, in fact, they are. The women aren't allowed to do anything. They just become baby machines. No school or anything. No sports. Is that any kind of life? Not that any of that matters to me. Why should it? As long as I'm not Muslim, that's all. I don't hate them for their clothes. I hate them because they're all first-class killers. They are a bloodthirsty lot who have nothing better to do than run around killing innocent people.

I know this for a fact. Cold-blooded fact. The blood that day was red and flowing. And real. There were so many, many people killed in that attack. Not that I could cry for them all. I mean, why should I? But there was one I didn't stop crying for. Still haven't stopped. I cry ever day. For my father—my beautiful, wonderful, loving father. Whose only fault was that he had gone to work. To earn a living so he could bring back goodies for us. Every day, he brought something special. And that day he'd promised to bring a chicken for dinner that night, because it was my mother's birthday. But . . . he never came back. There was a blast in the market in front of the temple and many people were blown to bits, including my handsome father. We never saw him again. Not even his body.

And so, I hate Muslims. Since that day, I hate them. I want nothing to do with them. If I could, I would kill a few myself. But I'm not Muslim, so I'm not into killing.

Anyway, after my father's death, there was no way we could continue to live in the same house, pretending that everything, everything, everything didn't remind us of him. And so we left. Moving to my Nana and Nani's house in another town. It wasn't easy. Not for me, but it was still nice to see my poor mother being looked after. She had completely lost the heart to do anything. Some days, getting out of bed was the best she could do. Then, she'd sit on the veranda and just stare. Nana was quite strict with me, but he let her be. He was forcing me to do things all the time. Lecturing me on how I had to be strong, carry on with my life. Study hard, do the best I could in school so that I could become independent and look after my mother in her old age. 'We are not going to be around forever,' he kept reminding. But he wouldn't say the same to his daughter and allowed Nani to stroke her head endlessly as my mother just lay in bed all day long.

So I went to the new school. The nearest one that would take me in. Luckily, I joined on the first day of the session and there were a few newcomers. So I wasn't noticed too much. We all sat in a circle to introduce ourselves. I noticed this really good-looking boy sitting across. He looked at me too and he smiled at me. Sort of. And I smiled back. Just a bit. I got a funny feeling in my stomach and had to look away, though I couldn't stop smiling. The names spun around me, Vandana, Bijoya, Priya, Vipin, Amar. I couldn't really remember them all. Besides, I was concentrating on the good-looking boy. That was one name I wanted to know. And remember. His turn was coming up. I leaned forward so I would catch it. Well, I caught it and dropped it immediately. Like it was a burning hot coal.

'Khalid,' he said. Khalid. A Muslim name.

I hated him immediately. I shot him a furious look.

Well, the rest of the session was a blur. For some reason we were not having classes that day. One of the old students explained that the first day was for everyone to have fun, relax and get to know each other better. I'd never been to a school like that. I kept trying to get the boy out of my head, but he kept creeping into my field of vision.

Then we were put into pairs and we had to enact an

impromptu play. And wouldn't you know it, I was lumped with Khalid. I was not going to have it. I wanted to change. I went up to the teacher. But one of the other girls was ahead of me and she was asking for her partner to be changed. 'No,' said the teacher, firmly shaking her head, 'no, no partner changes, sorry. And no exceptions,' she added a bit sharply as the girl tried to make her case. This was terrible. It sucked. I was stuck with the only Muslim in the class.

'What are you so angry about?' came a voice behind me. I whirled around. Of course it was Khalid, 'Hi, I'm Khalid and you're Nitya, isn't it?' he held out his hand, but I was damned if I was going to touch him.

'Hi,' I said, putting my hands firmly behind my back.

'Okay . . .' he smiled, looking at his hand as though he felt sorry for it. He had a really nice smile. I mean, a really, really nice smile.

'Behave yourself,' he said to his hand, 'can't you see that Nitya is angry and does not want to become friends right now?' he smacked his right hand with his left. 'Hand says sorry, hope you'll forgive it?'

I couldn't help the smile, but I did not want to get drawn by beautiful smiles and funny jokes. 'You hate this guy,' I had to remind myself.

'So, any ideas for the play we have to do?' I snapped at him. I mean, if he was going to be this all wise guy with snappy lines, he'd rather put it to better use than lame jokes.

'Hmm, how about a play about a really, really angry girl and a boy whose trying to figure out what she's angry about. As if he has NO idea.'

'Very funny!' I scowled.

'Why thank you,' he smiled back, 'I thought you'd like it. We can make it quite lifelike, you and I.'

I didn't quite know how to react to this. But, at the same time, I was not being able to come up with any bright ideas. So Khalid just started off, making up a story. And it was funny, very funny.

Everyone else had dispersed around the grounds and gardens to practise their plays. Khalid led me to a quiet spot, just behind a big bunch of some yellow flowers. I don't know what they were called, I'd never seen them before, but they were beautiful—glowing. And such a delicate, summery fragrance.

As we sat down, Khalid grinned and started to talk. He had a lovely voice. Deep, like a man's, not the boy voices that the others had. He spoke with music in his throat, as though the words all came out to a tune. And his eyes. Well, his eyes were like liquid honey. I couldn't help looking at those eyes. Even though I still hated him. I wished and wished and wished he wasn't Muslim.

'So,' he began, speaking softly, as though he was telling me a secret, 'so, for our play, any ideas? No?' he grinned and immediately started again, rightly assuming that I was not brimming with any ideas. 'There was this beautiful princess whose curly hair framed her head like a halo, so she looked like a princess of angels. But there was anger in her. A fire that burned deep and red. Many people came to try and put that anger out. Many tried to cool its heat with songs and music, food and dance. Handsome princes and wealthy kings came with kind words and offers of marriage. But did the princess' anger subside?'

He looked at me; was he asking me that question? 'No!' I said, trying to snap, but a smile on my face spoilt it.

'NO! You are quite right, nothing worked. But then, one day, a joker arrived. Oh he wasn't good looking or anything . . .'

'Yes, he was.'

'He was what?'

'He was good looking. Well, I mean, let's pretend that the joker was good looking.'

'Ah—a good-looking joker, huh? Okay, could you describe this joker, please?'

I scrabbled around, trying to describe something as far from Khalid as possible. But his honey eyes sparkled with amusement as though he could understand what I really meant. By now, I was pinching myself, reminding myself to hate this guy. I had to. Had to.

Khalid's face grew suddenly dark and clouded. He fell silent and dropped his lashes, shutting out his honey eyes.

What? Had I said something? But I hadn't, not out loud. I didn't know what to do, really. So we just sat there quietly.

And then he leaned forward, he picked up my hand. He rubbed the inside of my wrists. They were raw. I'd been pinching the soft skin there. It was a habit I'd got into after my father had died. Now, as Khalid rubbed the skin gently, the burning seemed to subside.

'You're really, really angry, aren't you?' he whispered so low that I had to lean forward to hear him, 'but why are you angry at me?'

He looked up and I noticed that his eyelashes were impossibly long. A boy shouldn't have such beautiful lashes. I couldn't help looking into those eyes. My heart fluttering, I didn't know what to say.

'I don't know why you're angry, but I really don't understand why you're angry at me. Tell me. Did I do something?'

What could I say? I couldn't tell him my anger could I? But I couldn't stop the tears either—his fingers were so soft on my raw wrists.

'My father died,' I sobbed. I'd never said this out aloud to anyone before. Never in those stark, unchangeable words.

'My father died. He was killed.'

'Who? Who did it?'

I looked at him. I hoped he'd understand.

'Muslims.' There, I'd said it and now we could hate each other forever.

He went all quiet. He took his hand away, although I wished he would continue soothing my wounds. But his hand was back in his own lap.

I was breathing hard. Panicking a bit. But he was closed.

All the banter gone now. I tried to think of something, anything to say. But nothing came to my mind and he would not look up. He had shut down. So we just sat there.

Finally, he said, in a low voice, 'Was it a Muslim or a terrorist that killed him?'

'How does it matter? He died.'

'It is not one and the same thing you know.'

'What?'

'Muslims and terrorists. It's not one and the same thing.'

'I don't care.' I was crying again.

'Well, you should, you must care. And you can't paint me with the terrorist brush either.'

'Why not, why not? My father is dead and it was a Muslim bomb that killed him.'

'My father is in the Indian Army and he is not a terrorist. He puts his life on the line every day. I live without him. Every day. Because he is trying to protect our country. He's trying to stop more Nityas from losing their fathers. And that is why you have to care. And you have to know the difference between Muslims and terrorists. Get it? I miss my father too.' He finished and I could see a hint of tears welling up in his gentle honey eyes.

He really did want me to, need me to understand. And I think I did, a little. At least I was beginning to. I think.

The spicy-sweet fragrance of the flowers lit up the air.

'Those flowers smell great, don't they?' I ventured, hoping to draw him back into the present.

But Khalid just nodded.

'What are these flowers called?' I was getting desperate. I was supposed to be the moody one, not him. Why was he getting all broody and silent?

But I just got a shrug out of him.

I leaned forward. I held his hands in mine. And then, without even thinking, I was on my knees and I kissed him on his cheek. We were both startled. I sat back down with a bump, my hand flying to my lips. Oh my god—if someone had seen us, I'd have been thrown out of school on my very first day. I looked around, but everyone was engrossed in their play. We'd been protected by the yellow flowers,.

I'd just kissed a boy. For the first time in my life, I'd kissed a boy. I looked at him. Was he angry? Did he hate it?

He smiled. He nodded. He put his hands over the wounds on my wrists and said, 'You've got to stop doing that, okay?'

Oh no! Did he mean the kiss? Oh no.

'I mean pinching your wrists. Hurting yourself. You've got to stop doing that. Okay?'

'Okay.' *Whew!*

'Promise?'

'Yes, promise.'

'So did the handsome joker make the princess smile?' I asked.

'Yeah, but in this fairy tale, it was the princess who kissed the joker and he turned into a frog . . .' he started hopping and croaking in a very poor imitation of a frog. I burst out laughing and couldn't stop.

'Yeah,' he said coming back, 'that's exactly how she laughed.'

We did our play for the class and we got huge laughs. Not that I actually kissed him again in front of everyone.

Well, we were a couple for quite a while. Right until the end of our school. Before he went on to join the army and I became a psychiatrist, a wife, a mother.

We kept up with each other for years and then lost touch. But just the other day, I got a whiff of a familiar fragrance. I followed the scent on the breeze until I reached a spot ablaze with a bush of yellow flowers. It was those very flowers of August.

Eid

AYUB CAME HOME from school in tears. Although his mother asked and asked and even tried to bribe him with his favourite gajar ka halwa, he was unwilling to tell her what had happened. Or maybe, he was unable to. It worried Ammi, she just didn't know what to do.

Eventually, Ayub calmed down and sat moodily munching his halwa. She decided not to drive him further into his silence by her questions. That afternoon, she let him watch cartoons before his homework. Something that happened very rarely. But she was relieved when he smiled and her heart sang out when she heard him giggle at the screen.

It was when Papa came home and they were sitting having their soup that Ayub finally came out with what was bothering him. 'Papa, are we Muslim?' he asked.

The soup went cold as Ayub told his parents about his day. About his days since the terrorist attacks in Mumbai. With the images of the Taj Hotel dome burning fresh in their minds, Ayub's classmates had started their teasing, taunting and yes. Even bullying. Ayub recalled all that had been happening to him.

'It's you guys who do this every time.'

'Every time.'

'You Mossies are just killers,'

'What do you eat for breakfast? Bodies?'

'Do you drink blood instead of milk?'

And then it had become worse. Shaan and his gang began teasing Ayub's friends, threatening them, warning them not to hang around with him any more. Every time they did, the others would pass by whispering, 'Traitor', 'gadaar' 'khalnayak' . . .

Eventually, only Shaurya had the guts to stick it out with Ayub. 'Just ignore them,' was his constant refrain.

But Ayub couldn't help tensing up every time there was another barb, another taunt flung his way.

But that day it had crossed all limits. Shaurya wasn't in school that day, he'd gone for a tennis match. So Ayub was alone, he took his lunch box and tried to quickly go to the furthest corner of the playground. Get away before they could follow. But they'd seen him. Shaan had gathered his cronies and a whole lot of others who joined in. Many because they were too scared to say no to Shaan, but others because they too actually believed that all Muslims were, in fact, terrorists, or at least sympathizers to their cause. That had been the talk in their homes, often.

They waited for Ayub to disappear behind the trees that bordered the walls.

'Good,' smirked Shaan to himself.

In fact, Ayub had made it much worse for himself. He'd not managed to escape the gaze of his tormentors, but had gone to an isolated spot where no one would see what was happening to him.

As he sat, lunch box open, but not eating, they came for him.

'Ah Mossie boy, so here you are!'

'You planning to blow up the school or something?'

'Enjoying your blood sandwich, are you?'

One of them snatched the tiffin box from his hand and opened the sandwich. They jeered as it was crumbled and thrown to the ground. They cheered as one of them stamped on the box until it snapped and smashed. From the corner of his eye, Ayub saw that his brownie had found its way into Shaan's pocket. Ayub tried to see if there was any escape for him. Could he make a dash for it? But there were too many of them. There was no way out.

No way out when Shaan caught hold of him from the back of his head. No way out when Shaan bent him over, rubbing his nose, his face into the ground. No way out as Ayub struggled for breath as he finally, finally sobbed out, as they demanded:

'I'm sorry, I'm sorry . . . I am a Muslim . . . I am a terrorist . . . I'm sorry I killed so many people.'

The laughing and hooting subsided as they left him sobbing and dirty on the ground behind the trees. From far away, he'd heard the bell ring for the end of the break. But his legs were shaking too hard. He couldn't stand for a long time. Finally, he'd managed to struggle to the bathrooms and wash his face. Not knowing what else to do. Knowing that there was no way he could go to the teachers and tell them what had just happened. That was out of the question. So he walked into class, late. Steeling himself for the inevitable taunting giggles that rose and for the scolding for being late.

'Speak up! I'm asking you a question—why are you so late for class?' the teacher demanded.

He just hung his head down, knowing that his silence was incensing the teacher more and more. But there was no answer he could give, so he mumbled a sorry and hoped it would be enough.

And then, through the afternoon, he was lost in thought, wondering how he was going to persuade his parents that he had to drop out of school, or at least transfer to another one. He took more scolding for being inattentive in his stride. That was the least of his problems.

But most of all, Ayub just couldn't figure out why they were picking on him. Was he different from all the others? And if yes, then, how?

Ayub added salty tears into the redness of his tomato soup. He couldn't bear it. He was the gentlest of children. He hated the way most boys would smack and knock each other 'just for the fun of it'. He couldn't see the fun in causing or receiving a painful whack.

He stayed clear of the rowdier boys and liked to play with girls, although he couldn't do that too much, because then the teasing became worse, he explained.

'They say, we should kill all the Muslims and only then will the world be peaceful.'

'That's what they say?' Papa and Ma looked at each other, horrified.

'Yes, and they say their parents say that too.'

Ayub's parents had always known that they would one day talk about religion with their son, but they hadn't thought it would be so soon, when he was just ten years old. They came from different religions themselves. He was Muslim and she was Christian. Neither family had accepted, or even forgiven them for falling in love. There had been bitter fights at their homes. Bordering on violence—almost.

No one from their families had attended the quiet court marriage that they'd had. They had never practised their religions after that. 'If it causes so much hatred, what good is it to go through the motions of praying to pieces of paper or stone statues?' they'd said. So they brought up their son without a religion. They celebrated birthdays, but no religious festivals. If he wanted to play Holi, or light candles at Diwali or get presents from Santa, he did. But they hadn't talked about the religious significance of what he was doing or that they were festivals of different religions.

They'd known this day would come, but yet, they weren't prepared at all to face it. And they hadn't imagined it would be brought up in such harsh circumstances.

They sat him down between them. They brought out family albums. Long ago ones that had pictures of his parents as children, each of them showing the religions of their backgrounds. 'This is a cross, beta; there is a story about how the Lord Jesus Christ was crucified on it because of his beliefs.'

'This is my first Eid, see how proud everyone is. I was the first son.'

They explained to him that officially he was half-Muslim and half-Christian. You have the best of two worlds, you know.

But the questions still remained. Why was he being taunted? And what did being half and half make him? And when they had said all that could be said about it, Ayub asked, 'So I am Christian and I am Muslim and that's okay? And I'm not going to be a killer, am I?' His very last question is what shook them the most, 'Why didn't you ever tell me about my religion before, were you ashamed of it?'

Ayub's parents knew that they were going to have to do something about it. Although he begged them not to, they went to school. They talked with the class teacher, the principal and some others. They were horrified too at what had happened. This school, like many others, had left the question of religion and discussion around it out of the curriculum. Out of the assembly prayers even, where they chose non-religious prayers for the general good of mankind. Policies they thought would be correct and healing and not bring about any conflict. But it hadn't turned out that way. Not at all.

The classes were addressed. The teachers thought it best to take a direct approach. Rather than just suspending the children, they wanted to try and convince them. Ayub's parents agreed. So now they stood before the class, the parents and teachers and principal together.

Ayub was nervous. Would his friends laugh? Would they be rude to him again? Or to his parents? Would they understand at all? Ayub's parents were worried too. Had they done the right thing in not talking about all of this earlier? Had they talked of it too soon? Would their son and his classmates really be able to comprehend all that they were about to say about such a complex thing as religion, and the similarities and differences? That religion only ever taught you to be a good human being? There was no religion that said you had to be a killer. There were bad people in any religion that killed and used their faith as an excuse. And so therefore it didn't matter what religion you were born with. One or more. Or any, for that matter.

One by one, they all read passages from different holy books—The Bible, the Koran, the Guru Granth Sahib, the Bhagvad Gita, and the Upanishads. They also talked about some of the difficulties they'd faced, being from different religions. About how they had come to be so wary that, in fact, they had never even shared with their own son what his religion was. That they celebrated festivals of all religions, but never talked about their religious significance, because they felt that it had started to breed violence and hatred in the world.

The class shifted uneasily. Shaan hung his head as others were glancing at him. He'd often picked on other kids, for all kinds of reasons. But he'd never had to face such a direct approach. He felt the reproach rise within him—for himself. And he could barely believe his ears when Ayub's mother extended the invitation. He looked up to see her smile at him as she said, 'So, we'd like to invite all of you to an Eid party. It will be Ayub's first official Eid. Here are the cards. We'd be very happy if your parents came too. I do hope that all of you will come.'

Finally, Ayub was dressed in his new white kurta pyjama. He wore his thread skull cap and he said his morning prayer on his brand new prayer mat. Kneeling alongside his father, watching from the corner of his eye as he bent forward and laid his forehead on the prayer mat, facing west, in the direction of Mecca.

Then he'd helped both his parents put the silver foil on the kheer, put raisins into the sevian. Put crisp notes of money into the new white envelopes for his friends' Eidi that he'd decorated himself.

And now it was time for the party to start.

When the first car drove up, Ayub felt almost faint with surprise, joy and terror. But his mother held his shoulder and gave him a small secret squeeze. They opened the door together to start celebrating Ayub's first Eid.

I Am Old and Tired Now . . .

I WAS SO drowned in my own miseries that I almost missed the story. My parents have been squabbling for the longest time—ever since I can remember. And I've always known somewhere that it would end like this. And yet, I've been unprepared. When they told me that they were getting a divorce, it was like a bolt out of the blue. Even though, I myself have told them more than a few times that they'd be better off living separately and so would I. But when the moment came and the boxes and suitcases came out, it was just, just terrible. I couldn't think of anything worse in life. It kind of made all my friends' whining and complaining about stupid things like not getting great food or not being allowed to go to some dumb party seem so petty and foolish. I know I became snappy and irritable with them. I don't know if they understood or not. But they started to keep away. Which was fine by me. Except, sometimes I really wanted to just sit and laugh over some inane thing or the other. But I didn't. I was moody and depressed and I didn't want to snap out of it, like my friends sometimes said I should. Why should I? They had no idea of the kind of misery I was in. The world around was black. No one was suffering more than I was. I felt old and tired.

But life, as they say, has to go on. There's no stopping it. So we carried on as though all was well. My parents went to their respective offices and I went unwillingly to school. Actually, school was kind of better than it had been, because there were no boxes and suitcases waiting for a new life, a new home there.

Anyway, it was English class, with Mrs Lal, my favourite teacher. We had this creative writing exercise. We were all handed pages of a newspaper. We had to pick out one story, any story. And we had to write a creative piece on it. I stared at it. Not really taking in any of it. Like I said, I was so wrapped in my own misery that I almost missed the story. It was the drawing of this ancient looking lion that really caught my eye. It was a beautiful line drawing, but it was the eyes that were striking. They were old, tired eyes, yet full of wisdom and a glint of something. Could it be hope? I read the piece. It was a story about the bombing of the Bamiyan Buddha statues. Of course I'd heard about that although it was a long time ago. But in the dust and rubble of the giant statues that were bombed by the Taliban in Afghanistan, there was also the bombing of the zoo. Somehow, these freaks of the Taliban had decided that zoos were ungodly, or something. Anyway, the zoo had got damaged and an old lion had escaped out of its cage. But nobody knew where it had gone. It disappeared and was never found again. Interesting. The image of the old lion came into my head. His eyes glowed with hope. Yes he was old, he was tired. But there was that glint. I started to write . . .

I am old and tired now.

There was a time, not so long ago, when I thought I had seen everything, experienced everything. Yet now, there are sounds and smells that are new.

But they are not happy ones. The smells are fearful, the sounds chill my blood and set these old bones rattling. There is no time, no pattern to their beginning. For it can catch you in the afternoon or rouse you from the deepest sleep of night. And the end is more frightful, more deafening. The absence more threatening than the presence.

I am old and tired now.

I've always resented this cage that has bound me ever since my capture from the forest where I roamed free. I was born to the king of that jungle and his most beautiful consort, my mother. My cub days were carefree. I had no fear for I was the favourite prince. But then, one day, the men came. My mother tried to warn me. But I ignored the ooh, ooh, ooh of her call, as she summoned me back to the safety of our den. I was curious. Something new lurked nearby and I had to find out what it was. It was too intriguing, I had to know.

And I did get to know. I now know about man and his traps and nets. I know about cages and zoos. I know about children who rouse you by shouting and throwing stones at you. I know altogether too much about man and his way—perhaps not enough about being a real lion.

Some may think that this is a life of comfort, having food brought to you without having to hunt, having a home without having to fight for territory. But no lion would choose the life of a cage over a life of freedom—whatever the hardships. I grew up in a cage, surrounded by man. Slowly I got to understand their ways, their language. My keepers were kind enough and over a period of time, I came to get used to this life. But I was never happy.

But I'm old and tired now.

And yet there are things anew—smells and sounds that evoke fear. I hear new words too—words like 'war' and 'bombs' and death hangs heavy in the air. What does man fight over, I wonder?. Is it territory and food as in the ways of the jungle? But there is so much land for man. And he can make his own food. There must surely be enough for all.

Soon the sounds and smells creep closer and closer to this cage I call home. Until one day, fire falls from the sky and there is death and destruction everywhere. The cries of gibbons and giraffes. The wails of kangaroos and koalas rent the air. I find the bars of my cage shattered. I cower in a corner of my torn cage and wait. And wait. But my keepers do not come any more. My body demands to be fed and I know that I must eat before my body becomes too weak to find sustenance.

I step out of my cage. I am surrounded by the dead and dying. But I do not eat them, for they bear a strange smell about them. I walk on beyond the shattered walls of the zoo. There is something in the air that stirs my memories. The lure of a forest and river propels me forward. I know now that I can be free of man. Fighting man.

I walk and walk through days and nights.

I am old and tired now, but my legs and heart have the youth of hope firing them. Giving me the will to walk. Through days and nights.

There is the scent of green and water. A forest lives nearby. My senses, buried under years of captivity, break free and make my heart sing. I break into a run. Freedom beckons.

I am old and tired but I will be free. I will live free. In peace.

I felt myself tearing up. I hoped no one was going to notice. But I felt the lion's spirit inside me. I know that sounds pretty weird. I know that if I was to share that thought with anyone, even my friends, they'd condemn me for good. But I felt, I don't know . . . I felt, if the lion could have gone through all that—war and bombing and could still find hope. And peace. Then maybe I could too. Maybe things were not so bad. Maybe all that was happening was for the better and I'd get a peaceful home at last.

I sat back, kind of exhausted by the journey of the lion. And myself. And after a long time, I smiled.

Waiting

SHE WAITED. AN unease starting to filter its presence into her although it really wasn't yet time for him to come home. Not as yet. He was a creature of habit and she was too. They lived together comfortably within the steady drumbeat of their well-ordered lives. They awoke early and he fed her—not food out of a packet, but fresh, cooked every morning while he had his tea. Then they walked together for about half an hour, enjoying the freshness of early mornings before the air became stale with heat and bodies rushing about their daily business. She liked to see the children rushing off to school. Some were frightened of her, but there was one girl who would come up and pat her on her head. She liked that.

Then back home again and he'd have his breakfast, giving her little bites from his food. Just little tokens of his affection.

At first she had hated being left alone in the flat. She had tried everything to stop him from leaving. But now, she knew that he did have to go and she didn't mind it so much any more. For now she knew that he would always come back. She slept and looked out of the window, waiting, always waiting for signs of him. She enjoyed seeing the busyness of the ant-like people far down below. She wondered why they always rushed so much; they never meandered—never stopped to talk to one another. Or look at something for the pleasure of it. Sometimes their rushing made her almost dizzy. Then she would curl up on their favourite sofa, the one that they sat and watched TV on in the evenings. She liked it there. It was safe and cool under the whirring fan that he always left on for her so she would not mind the heat so much. Once he'd even offered to leave the air conditioner on, but she was glad that he didn't. It stiffened her old bones. She liked it on the sofa too because it held the scent of him. As she slept, she could feel his presence and often dreamt that she was lying with her great head in his comforting lap. She adored him and he her.

But now he was late. He was hardly ever late. Just once, in fact, when it had rained all night and he had been unable to get home. He had spent the night in the car and she had been wild with worry. It was a night that she never wanted to repeat. Even though he had taken leave the next day and spent the whole day with her in his arms. But the nagging worry that he would not return had taken a long, long time to heal. Before his endless promises that he would never leave her alone again another night finally convinced her that she was safe. That he would return. She held this promise close to her heart.

Then why was he not home yet? She sat with her nose pressed to the window. For so long that the whole window was so fogged up that she couldn't see out any more. But she had already seen the rush and crush of people. It had a different rhythm that night. There seemed to be more urgency, more panic in the way the ant-people moved that night. And then, just as suddenly as the rushing began, it seemed to stop. It was as if it was now very, very late at night, although it wasn't, not yet. The streets were emptied of all life. Even the dogs outside seemed to have quit their incessant barking and quarrelling. She never barked back at them. It was beneath her dignity.

Where, oh where could he be? The panic started to eat into her like termites, gnawing from the outside in. First she felt the panic set in her old bones. She felt as though her skeleton had turned to dust. She couldn't stand up any more. Her legs wouldn't hold her up. So she lay down on the sofa and tried to sleep, but the termites of panic were moving up towards her skin until it crawled with mites of fear, prickling her and making her hackles stand on end. Back to the window, looking out. But there was nothing to see. Only a strange orange glow filled the sky. Foreboding thickened her blood.

Lost, he was lost. A voice deep in her primeval being told her.

He is gone.

He is not coming back.

Her throat tightened with the loss that she suddenly became aware of. She had lost him. He would not, could not return. Her throat squeezed in on itself and she let out a howl so painful that the very air in the apartment seemed to freeze into a dread stillness. The howl escaped her again. And again. And she was weeping . . . he would not return . . .

The television has been blaring non-stop since early in the morning. Since the terrorist attacks on Mumbai started. Our building is still and silent. The usual gathering of kids playing in the garden and the old people sitting on benches hasn't happened today. It was the same yesterday. My head's hurting from the sounds of terror blasting into our lives from every TV. I wish they'd switch to some other channels. I tried to tell my parents. I think it would do them some good to watch something fun and light. But they're glued to bad news, as is the rest of our society. I mean, I can understand that you want to know what's happening in your city. But come on, beyond a point, you've got to get back to your own lives. I mean, I'm sorry for those people who have died, but, you know, we're *alive, let's behave as though* we *haven't been caught in the crossfire too. I tried to tell my mom, but she just scowled. In fact, I tried to tell my best friend Riya, but she called me callous. I'm NOT callous. I just think that there's no good to be got from depressing yourself further. Things are bad enough in our own lives, without needing to obsess over someone else's bad news. Somehow my parents do not agree with this point of view. So now they're insisting that we go for a prayer meeting being held by our society. I had really wished* that they'd go so I could lighten my own mood by watching some mindless TV. But that wasn't happening. So I went.

And that's when I got a shock. Someone from our building. Our own building seemed to have died in the riots. Mr Ranade. A sweet man really. He lived alone, not talking too much to anyone, but wishing everyone politely. He was one of the few older people who didn't yell at the children for playing with a ball or anything. He only smiled when we looked at him. Sometimes we wished him too. He led a very regular life. Fetching his milk when we were going to school, walking his dog in the evening.

Oh my god—the dog! The dog, what had happened to the dog? None of us had remembered about her. She was a sweet thing. A stray that the old man had rescued when she was a puppy, I think. Her name was Laila. An unusually romantic name for such a simple, quiet man. I remembered we'd laughed, sniggered, when he'd told us her name. I also remembered that he'd said it shyly. Almost blushing. But we'd sniggered behind his back. Later, though, it was nice to see the two of them, going out for their walk. I liked to pat Laila's soft head sometimes.

And now we'd forgotten all about the dog. How could we have? In the din and chaos that followed the Mumbai terror attacks, no one had had mind space for a dog.

I ran to my parents now and they got the spare key from the president. My parents didn't want me to come along. I knew it was because they thought the dog might have died from starvation. But I sneaked in after them.

She was as thin as a stick, her ribs sticking out, her face gaunt.

But she was alive. Before anyone could stop me, I ran over to her and put my arms around her. Murmering my apologies to her. That I'd forgotten all about her. But she licked my face and feebly wagged her tail and seemed to whisper something soft into my ear.

And that's when I started to cry. For the first time since the attacks, I cried. For something that was not mine. It was not a personal pain. But something in Laila's ability to forgive me for forgetting and thanking me for remembering her made me realize that I wasn't the centre of the universe after all. There was life out there, and I needed to care.

Yes, my parents allowed me to take Laila in. She recovered slowly, gaining back a little weight, a little light in her sad eyes, a little happiness in the shake of her tail. She followed me everywhere, afraid that I would leave her too. But I never left her. For she had opened my eyes.

Read More in Puffin

BOLLYWOOD KNIGHTS: SHOOT THE PEACOCK

by Nick Raposo

There was a twanging sound, and she felt her harness shudder. Reality seemed to slow down, as she looked up at the crane and saw her wire falling away, down into the gorge.

It's hard being the only son of a Bollywood superstar, and seventeen-year-old Raj Kapoor's life just got a little bit more complicated. Preeti Shabbir, the beautiful starlet acting in Amit Kapoor's latest film, is almost killed in a suspicious accident on the set. Raj and his friends Nagi and Madhuri resolve to find the would-be killer and stop him before he tries to finish the job. But is Preeti the intended victim? Or is the killer's aim something even more chilling?

In the first book featuring the detective trio from Mumbai's glittering film world, *Shoot the Peacock* will take you on a wild ride through the fabulous and mysterious world of Bollywood at work and at play.

Read More in Puffin

BOLLYWOOD KNIGHTS: SHOOT THE CROW

by Nick Raposo

She had a pang of guilt as she walked to the door. She had told only one person what she was doing, and even then not the whole truth. She certainly hadn't mentioned the gun. The reality was that she might well never see anyone from this life again.

Teen detectives Raj, Nagi and Madhuri are drawn into a web of deceit when Ameeta Soares, a rising Bollywood star, disappears from her swank Malabar Hill apartment. When the missing actress is accused of a brutal murder, the trio must plumb the depths of Mumbai's underworld in a desperate attempt to track her down. Along the way, they play a dangerous game and end up in the sights of a cold-blooded killer.

Who is the Crow, determined to eliminate Ameeta? And whose is the shadowy hand directing the Crow's every move? The Bollywood Knights embark on a roller-coaster ride which takes them from the glamorous hangouts of Bollywood stars to seedy back-alley dance bars till the final, heart-stopping showdown.

Read More in Puffin

DOA DETECTIVE FILES: TROUBLE AT THE TAJ

by Sonja Chandrachud

'Natural or supernatural
No mystery is out of this world for us . . .'

Travel back in time with the DOA gang as they solve out-of-this-world mysteries using their wits, will and Tuk Tuk, their auto rickshaw with attitude, which also happens to be a time machine!

DOA Case File 1
Agra, India, 1636: There's some serious trouble at the Taj!

Chief architect of the Taj Mahal, Ustad Ahmed Lahauri, has been kidnapped, leaving work on the construction unfinished. Emperor Shah Jahan now has to find a new architect for his dream project. But the ghost of his dead empress, Mumtaz Mahal, is determined not to let any other architect work on her mausoleum. She summons the DOA detectives and commands them to find the missing architect before it's too late and she's saddled with a hideous tomb for eternity.

Soon the detectives discover that there is much more to the Ustad's disappearance than a mere kidnapping. There is a traitor in the imperial court who will stop at nothing till he fulfils his evil designs! Who could it be? Will the detectives be able to stop his wicked plans? Will they be able to ensure that the magnificent Taj Mahal gets built?